Colleen H. Robbins

Night Breeze and Moonbeams:

Stories and Poems of Myth, Magic, and the Medieval

Daraga Flight Publishing

2022 Daraga Flight Publishing

Some of the contents have previously appeared in print. An extended copyright page appears after the text.

Published in the United States of America by Daraga Flight Publishing.

ISBN 978-1-7320803-5-5

Cover Art copyright Rafael Ramos
Cover Assembly Kenneth McGee
Printed in the United States of America

Visit www.DaragaFlight.weebly.com

The hunter blocked her path. "Have you ever found anything else out there?"

"Pretty feathers from the birds."

He narrowed his eyes. "What about a unicorn's horn?"

Talia looked up at his neck. She spotted the scar and smiled. "Do you mean a long white twisty horn from a white horse?" She drew her hands apart, tracing a spiral with one finger.

"Yes, that's exactly right. Did you see a unicorn?" He practically danced with excitement.

"No, but I saw a horn once. My brother found it. He took it into the city to sell it last fall, but he didn't come back yet.".

"Where did your brother find the horn? Can you show me?"

"He found it in Grandpa's old trunk, along with some rusty swords and armor." Talia prattled on like her youngest sister. "Grandpa caught a white unicorn and gave it to a king a long time ago. The king killed it a week later. Silly king."

--Ugly Horses

Books by Colleen H. Robbins

THE DARAGA SERIES
Daraga's Quest
Daraga's Children
Dark Protector

COLLECTIONS
Stories of a Sheltered Suburbanite
Night Breeze and Moonbeams: Stories of Myth, Magic, and the Medieval

ANTHOLOGIES including stories by CHR
Bombshells: Stories and Poems by Women on the Homefront (ed. M. Martin, J. Loren)
Krampusnacht: 12 Nights of Krampus (ed. Kate Wolford)
Eldritch Embraces: Putting the Love Back in Lovecraft (ed. Micheal Cieslak)
Write Where We Are: 2017 (Write On! Joliet)
Write Where We Are: 2018 (Write On! Joliet)
Cheetah Stories (Write On! Joliet)
Write Where We Are: 2019 (Write On! Joliet)
Write Where We Are: 2020 (Write On! Joliet)
Write Where We Are: 2021 (Write On! Joliet)

COLLABORATIONS
Return to Ganagar (with Tarina Jameson)

:

.

Dedicated to my husband,

my children,

my grandchildren,

Cherish Hunter who wanted to see rainbows,

And to my friend Gerald Warfield,

Who passed at too young an age.

Colleen H. Robbins

\#

NIGHT BREEZE and MOONBEAMS:

Stories and Poems of Myth, Magic, and the Medieval

by Colleen H. Robbins

Colleen. H. Robbins

Table of Contents

Introduction

There are historical re-creation groups that deal with Ancient Cultures (such as Assyro-Babylonian, Egyptian, and Oriental), the Medieval Period (from the legends of King Arthur and Camelot, the fall of the Roman Empire, Vikings, and the Crusades), and the Renaissance with their elaborate costumes, including the rediscovery of ancient Greek and Roman tales of fantastic creatures. These unicorns, gryphons, mermaids, and other creatures, soon took their place in the legends and stories of the time, and were emblazoned (painted) on shields.

Being a fan of mythology, and a member of such groups, I enjoyed the revels (parties) and weekend long camping events that usually included a tournament (fighting competition with armor and helmets), a feast of medieval-inspired foods, and some form of scheduled entertainment (songs, stories, demonstrations of skill). Occasionally we observed a rare joust between armored knights on horseback. Participants wore costumes that fit their persona (a made-up character who could have lived during the time period... with no actual historic figures}. Some events also included mini classes in everything from Courtly Dances and costuming, to calligraphy (fancy writing styles) and historical information on particular time periods.

The Medieval and Renaissance re-creation later led to the early Renaissance Faires, now popular throughout the United States.

I also write Fantasy, Science fiction and Horror, so some of the included stories cross over. You'll find modern folk meeting with mythological creatures, and even a set of stories where a wizard transports modern re-enactors back through time... and the legends they spawn. Enjoy! -CHR

Ugly Horses

The March wind swirled with old leaves and new snow. Talia flipped the tangled mess of her hair back from her face. She should probably brush it again one of these weeks. She shook her head. Summer came in a few more months; she could just cut it off with Mama's old knife and grow it again. She poked a long stick into the leaves and dug down when she felt something hard. She came up with a cast-off deer antler, thick at the bottom and three points on top. Only a few nibbles chipped the bottom. What a find! She tucked it into the leather bag that hung from her shoulder. The blacksmith loved good antlers; they made excellent hilts for his knives. He might even pay her for it, or at least deduct part of the money she owed him for investigating her brother's murder. *Someday she would find the hunter with that star-shaped scar.*

She passed through the edges of the meadow. Ducking down near a raspberry thicket to dig, she caught sight of a pair of spotted fawns half buried in the leaves beneath the thorns. She smiled and waved at them. This time her digging produced two matching antlers, each with five points and untouched.

The next hour she added three more antlers to her bag, all of them badly nibbled. If the deer and other animals nibbled at the cast-offs, it meant that they were getting ready to grow this year's antlers. This would be her last collecting trip for the year. The forest and meadows would soon be too dangerous to travel, mostly because of the ugly horses.

Thin legged and thick necked, they walked with their heads drooping down. Only the youngest foals walked with their heads up, and that changed when they shed their baby coat.

Talia was lucky enough to see an ugly horse pawing through the snow in the edge of the meadow before it saw her. A second stood nearby while a black and dark brown spotted foal nursed. She tossed two of the badly nibbled antlers in their direction, just in case, but they ignored her. Shaggy clumps of matted winter fur hung from the adults' bellies. She glanced around to see if the rest of the herd approached, but they were likely still by the river at this time of year. She headed back to the meadow.

The crunch of dead leaves sounded off to the side. She slowed for a moment, then continued as she identified the pattern of human footsteps.

The hunter's bow, a quiver of red-feathered arrows, and a pretty set of matched knives stood out against his green and brown clothing. He caught up to her as she reached the rutted road back to the farm.

"You. Little girl. Stop." His voice sounded raw in the dry air.

Talia kept walking, clutching her collecting bag close. With four sisters, her family needed the money that the antlers would bring. The younger girls kept a large vegetable and herb garden that helped during the summer, and the apples and grapes helped in the fall, but the early spring antler collecting allowed Talia to buy the medicines that their father still needed. The herd caught him last summer on a too-sunny day.

"I told you to stop." The hunter laid a hand on her shoulder. "What do you have in your bag?"

"It's mine." She curled over the bag and hugged it. *Could he be the one?*

The hunter jerked the bag away and dumped it on the ground. All four remaining antlers fell out, as well as some leftover moss Talia found hanging from a tree. ""What is this? No money, no weapons, and too small to be of use. Why did you put these in your bag?"

"Antlers make nice hilts for knives." She grabbed her bag back and carefully wrapped the moss around the antlers as she placed them inside.

"Do you wander these woods a lot?"

"Enough. But I need to get home."

He blocked her path. "Have you ever found anything else out there?"

"Pretty feathers from the birds. But that won't be until summer."

He narrowed his eyes. "What about a unicorn's horn?"

Talia looked up at his neck. She spotted the scar and smiled. "Do you mean a long white twisty horn from a white horse?" She drew her hands apart, tracing a spiral with one finger.

"Yes, that's exactly right. Did you see a unicorn?" He practically danced with excitement.

"No, but I saw a horn once. My brother found it. He took it into the city to sell it last fall, but he didn't come back yet." *But he couldn't, could he,* she thought.

"Where did your brother find the horn? Can you show me?"

"He found it in Grandpa's old trunk, along with some rusty swords and armor." Talia prattled on like her youngest sister. "Grandpa caught a white unicorn and gave it to a king a long time ago. The king killed it a week later. Silly king."

"And where did your grandfather catch it? Near here?"

"No, silly, in the mountains. It took him almost a year, that's what Papa says."

"Oh. Well, did you see any deer while you were collecting?"

"No." She drew out the word as she looked over her shoulder at the forest trail. "But I know where they are." Talia started to cry. "If I tell you, then you and your friends will just kill them."

He patted her lightly on the shoulder. "No, I'm all alone, little girl. I won't kill more than one."

She pulled her arm away. Hot tears stung her eyes, tears of rage. How dare her brother's murderer pat her the

7

same way her brother used to? How arrogant this hunter, coming all alone. Worst of all, he kept calling her little. She was short, yes, shorter than most of her younger sisters, but she was no fool. She looked at her footprints in the snow.

"Do you promise?" At his nod, she continued. "They stay down by the river. If you go across the meadow, there's a trail that goes a couple of miles through the trees. I'm not allowed to go that far, so I only went partway down it."

"At least I haven't wasted a trip." He turned and headed back toward the meadow. "I'll bring you back an antler if I find one."

Talia forced a smile as she continued up the road to the farm. He wouldn't be back. Her grandfather told her father the secret of the ugly horses, and Papa told her.

"They need to eat antlers and bones to grow nice strong horns each year. Once they cast their spiral horns and start shedding their winter fur, they start hunting. They'll eat rabbits and deer if they must, but they really like the taste of human flesh."

And Grandpa brought back a lot more than the rare albino that he gave to the king. A small herd, just enough to keep the deer under control, lived in the woods now. She wondered if the hunter's knives would rust before the next time it rained, when the ugly horses didn't hunt or eat. The blacksmith might pay her extra for such a pretty matched set.

Gryphon Lore

With eagle's head and eagle's wings—
Of lion's body, tail, and claws—
The gryphon lore speaks of such things
And follows with its own strange laws.

For those who wish to feel the breeze
Beneath their feather'd wings of brown
And glide and soar above the trees
Before returning to the ground,

There is a potion of great might--
'Twas told of by a mighty djinn--
Which gives the bear'r the gift of flight
When holding feathers dipped within.

The kettle seethes and stirs and boils;
The feathers are of gryphons true;
Ingredients gained from great toils,
And I shall name them all to you:

An eagle's foot, a lizard's claw,
A whisker of a lion small,
Must boil with a small dragon's paw
And cook beneath an oak tree tall.

From one full moon until the next,
The kettle must be simmered well,
And reading from this ancient text,
You must pronounce the changing spell:

"O Gryphon strong, I would be thee,
For else I must the ground stay by,
I ask beneath the old oak tree
As moonbeams shine and cold winds sigh.

"My skin will plump and feathers grow,
And I will leap into the air
And watch my earth-bound family go,
As I fly here and I fly there."

The danger lies, the lore does warn,
That one may grow forgetful yet
And keep the shape of gryphons born;
His name and family he'll forget.

And finally, says the gryphon tome,
His feathers he will drop to ground,
And freedom's flight leaves him alone,
And weeping, he'll cry that he's bound.

Whispering Robes

Whispering robes down forest path
Together in silence they go
The full moon rises, the oak trees lean
To hear them speak, for they know.

Chantings of cadence, rising to songs
Bespeak to some truth, to some woe
Throughout the night it all continues
Golden sickle flashing, thud of mistletoe.

Deep thought by some on what they hath
And what they gave up, such as sword and bow
The worth of the new life is greater, they say,
For we shall truly reap whatever we sow.

Chirping of birds prepare for dawn
Whispering robes turn to go
Forest noises return, filling the silence:
They've left to finish with plow and hoe.

Colleen H. Robbins

She Dances For No Man

The dancer, she dances for no man, that one.
She dances for memory, face bright in the sun.
And she dances for you, you glance at her eyes.
The face mirrored is different; 'tis where her heart lies.

She dances before you as you sit, so lightly.
Her thoughts turning inward to a young man so sprightly.
Make the wrong move, she twists, turns, spins—then gone…
To dance for another man… and the dance goes on.

You sit there, and watch to see where her eyes rest
To get an idea of what she likes best,
And a picture builds up right before your own eyes,
A picture of he—where her heart truly lies.

A tall man, a slim man, his hair just that shade
Of the sand in the stream where the young children wade.
The strength is there, hidden, muscles not overlarge,
Like the fellow you met once on an old river barge.

And then you remember what she can't forget.
The battlefield: scarlet blood stains the ground yet.
The birds circling low on that hot summer's day,
Circling close to the fellow, his soul flown away.

And she turns back to you once again in her dance,
Trying not to remember her man's death by lance,
And her eyes mirror back that same face that you knew.
She knows you remember--it could have been you.

The Lure

Derek pulled himself out of the water and staggered up the rocky beach. The cold wind howled, numbing him. He focused his eyes on a thick knot of bushes up the beach, pointed his body toward them, and let his mind slip back to yesterday.

With sunny weather and calm seas, it was perfect weather for sailing. Derek planned to sail between St. Croix and Bermuda for years, but something always came up to change his plans. This time it was the girl in the long red skirt.

She seemed so alone, sitting at the end of the little bar in Christiansted. *One pale face in a sea of darkness*, he thought. Derek was enchanted at his first sight of her. He'd been smooth, talking with her and observing all the customs, at least long enough to lure her to his hotel room.

She'd gone willingly enough, and she stood in the doorway scanning the room with an intensity that surprised him. Her eyes stopped on the little frame sitting on his nightstand.

"Oh, a sailboat!" she cried out in a voice that reminded him of seagulls squawking. Her voice dropped to a murmur. "Is it yours?"

"Thirty-six foot Pearson, and her inboard motors are powerful enough for waterskiing. I named her *Mystique*." Derek warmed to the topic of his boat and spent the better part of an hour telling his fascinated guest about his travels. Realizing suddenly that he wasted time, he tried to steer the conversation back to the girl. "So, why sit all alone in the bar?" *Oh, wonderful, Derek. Let's be blunt*, he chastised himself.

"My life is boring. I thought if I sat there long enough, some wonderful adventure would find its way to me." She cocked her head to one side and stared at him with wonderfully large green eyes. "And I think it has." She smiled at him, and Derek was enchanted again.

"Would you like to go sailing with me? I've got the boat all stocked up and ready to go. We'll make our own adventure. Derek licked his lips with anticipation.

The girl laughed, her voice ebbing and flowing like waves crashing on the rocks. Derek thought an undercurrent of bitterness tinged the sound, but it washed away in the sheer joy of her next wave of laughter. Without speaking, they gathered the few things he stored in the hotel room, left the key on the bureau, and slipped away to the marina. In less than an hour, they set sail.

Derek checked his charts and headed for the open ocean. They sailed just out of sight of land when the squall hit. It blew up out of a clear sky, or maybe he was too involved thinking about his plans for the girl. The wind lashed at his sails. The thousand duties necessary to keep the *Mystique* from swamping distracted Derek from his thoughts.

The winds increased, howling past his ears, singing through the rigging as the sails tore to shreds. He fought to see through the driving rain, worried that the storm might drive him too close to the myriad islands. The winds gusted from the side, surprising him, and he felt a grinding vibration through the hull of the boat as she landed on something solid. Waves broke over the side, pushing the *Mystique* further onto the obstruction. The mast broke with a sharp *crack*, knocking Derek over the side of the boat and into the waiting arms of the sea. He grabbed at his lifejacket and watched it swirl on past, washing further from his reach with each wave that hurried by.

Derek stopped suddenly as he walked into the knot of bushes. He shivered again and pushed boldly through the greenery. A moment later he looked down the far side of the tiny island at the waves crashing on the farther shore. He heard the girl's laugh and realized he'd forgotten to ask her

14

name or even think about her in the midst of the storm. He turned to follow the sound.

The bright red of her skirt rolling in the green waves at the water's edge caught his eye, just as the girl had when they first met. She laughed again, and he raised his eyes, tracking the sound until he saw movement. The girl laughed and played in the water beyond with her sister mermaids, their scaly legs as green as their eyes, leaping like dolphins in the rolling surf.

Colleen H. Robbins

Leprechauns Cobbling

Leprechauns cobbling,
Tapping away,
Cobbling the night long,
Sleeping by day.

Faeries aflutter
Fly here and there,
Tiny moss flowers
Pinned in their hair.

Will-o-wisps floating
Over the mires,
Luring poor trav'lers
Far from their shires.

Springtime is 'wakening
Throughout the land;
Weather is warming—
Wintertime banned.

The Alchemist Syndrome

The Alchemist Syndrome: don't we all know
They're turning lead bars right into bright gold.

The sorcerers wail
Of their rivals' success.
Despairing, they simply
Ask for redress.

"Half of the gold that you made," goes their cry,
"Else we will be paupers and surely will die."

But one old sorcerer
Crafty old soul
Buys cheap lead bars
As his one seeming goal.

"Traitor! Turncoat!" His brethren do shout.
"You closet alchemist! Put him out! Put him out!"

They listen to nothing
The old man does say
So he turns in his hat
And bids them "Good Day."

A short ten years later or perhaps 'tis thirteen
Gold all around but no lead to be seen.

And now the old sorcerer
His crafty smile bold
Sells lead to the alchemists
For one hundred weight gold.

Colleen H. Robbins

My Young Son

The first sword swing of my young son
A moment proud for me
The first sword swing of my young son
For his father's gone to sea

The first bow shot of my young son
A buck he did bring down
The first bow shot of my young son
We fed near half the town

The first sweet tryst of my young son
He's grown near to a man
The first sweet tryst of my young son
He'll soon have his own land

The first young son of my young son
Though all grown up he be
The first young son of my young son
And my son has gone to sea

Changelings

02 June 2008, 7:00 pm

A child is missing. Mickey O'Neill this time, just another red-haired five-year-old with a sprinkling of freckles. The third lost child this year. Groveton, Missouri isn't big enough to lose as many children as we do, but what five-year-old child in the Ozarks can resist exploring the forest? The rangers of the Mark Twain Forest know us all by name now.

Granny Eileen had her own ideas. We're an old community here, settled back before the first railroad workers came through. Our ancestors brought their families, their hound dogs, and their beliefs. They even brought their pookas with them. Granny Eileen always said the pookas lure the children away so they can be replaced with changelings, but Granny Eileen said a lot of things. Mostly she said that a thirty-one year old woman as pretty as I am should settle down and get married instead of working as a sheriff's deputy. Don't let her fool you. Mousy-brown hair and a boy-slender figure aren't anyone's idea of pretty except hers.

It's getting dark now, and the flashlights are starting to shine like fireflies in the back yard. There must be a hundred and fifty people out searching by now. Where are they all coming from? We'll find the boy before the night is over. We always do when they're young. Even if he's not really the same boy.

August 1982

Cold water, colder than I expected, made my fingers tingle. Leslie squealed as she stuck her toe in. We weren't neither of us supposed to be in the water, but it was too hot to wait for Daddy to come back from visiting his parole officer. I didn't really want to wait for him, anyhow. If he saw me swimming nekkid, he might want to play the game again. I didn't like it much, especially the new rule about hiding things. I still hurt from the last time we played. The cold water made my stomach feel better.

"Alanna, I got a secret."

I leaned closer so Leslie could whisper it to me. We didn't want the frogs to hear us. They're terrible gossips. Granny Eileen says so, and she knows everything.

"My Daddy started playing the game with me last night."

"Did it hurt?" She nodded. I frowned. "What are we gonna do?" I crawled up the bank and sat down on the leaves next to the old basket with our lunch. Leslie and I shared all our secrets, even the ones that we weren't supposed to tell. I started to cry. My stomach felt worse than ever.

Leslie plopped down next to me and hugged me. "I'm gonna run away to Saint Louis. My Momma's cousin lives up there. She isn't married, so there won't be a Daddy around. I'm gonna grow up to be a movie star."

"I wish I could go with you. Momma's gonna have a baby any day and she needs me to help."

"You can come visit later after the baby gets born. Ouch!" Leslie jumped up and danced around. "Something's biting my butt." She brushed away a bunch of ants. Two held on tight.

I helped her pick the last two ants loose. We shook out our clothes, put them on, and then Leslie took the basket and walked up to the road. I sat by the river and watched as a car stopped and she got inside. I hoped she found her cousin in the city.

Momma screamed when I got home, and not just cause she was mad. I ran to find the midwife. Lots of people shouted and ran around like crazy because someone was missing. By the time I figured out they meant Leslie, they already found her. Right in the Mark Twain Forest, just like all the other kids.

02 June 2008, 7:45 pm

I couldn't help thinking about all those other missing children. Groveton, population 512, is the capital for runaways. There are two groups that run away most: the five-year-olds and the teenagers. Too often, they are the same kids. To save ourselves the paperwork, we just leave the files open after the little ones are found.

It didn't surprise Granny Eileen when I figured out the pattern. She said that's what changelings do. They always run away when they've been discovered. I don't remember anyone else except Granny talking about changelings and pookas, though. If they were discovered, wouldn't someone say something? I wondered for a long time why the pookas took the kids. Granny said they want to break our hearts. The mothers of the little ones cry so hard while we're looking. The mothers of the teenagers don't hardly cry at all.

September 1985

I stopped and got Leslie on the way to the school bus every day, just out of habit. We weren't really friends any more, not since the summer she ran away. Third grade was so hard. Both of us huddled in our towels after gym class at school.

The teachers made us take a shower every single time. Did they think I would get them dirty? I already took my bath in the river that week. Mostly I worried that someone would see the bruises or the blood that sometimes happened after Daddy's games.

Leslie's towel slipped that day when she faced away from me. I wondered if she had the same kind of bruises. I stared so long the other kids noticed and started to tease me. I shut my mouth. What could I say? I saw Leslie's little two-inch hairless tail hanging down. My friend Leslie who ran away didn't have a tail, just ant bites. The Leslie they found wasn't the same girl.

I spent all day convincing myself that Leslie didn't have a tail. My mind wouldn't let it rest. By the time I got home from school, I ran in completely panicked. I ran up Sommers Street, right past Mrs. Smithy when she tried to ask me where Leslie was, and barreled past my little sister Peggy like a hundred monsters snapped at my heels.

Her pink purse went spinning across the floor, and Peggy started bawling.

I ran up to Momma and clung to her waist. "I don't want Daddy's thing to break off in me and hang out like a tail. Make him stop the games, Momma, please!"

02 June 2008, 8 pm

I looked again at Mickey's school picture. It's a good thing we photograph the children twice a year at school. His emerald green eyes sparkled with mischief. A strand of wavy red hair fell across his forehead.

My radio crackled. Sheriff Teague's wheezy voice rolled out through the static. "Alanna, Ranger Everett needs to talk with you over at the station."

"Can you patch it through? My car's parked about three miles back."

"Nope, he needs to see you in person. Nothing we want to put over the radio."

I felt a cold shiver. "It's not the little boy, is it?" I could picture him lying under a bush like a rag doll, the way so many of the outsider children were found.

"Something else entirely. Go on, there's plenty of searchers out there."

"Tell Nick I'll be there as soon as I can. Maybe an hour."

I walked back through the darkened fields. My flashlight beam didn't compensate for the lack of moonlight. Thick clouds rolled across the sky, and the wind rustled through the leaves of the bushes. All the meadow grass was tromped flat, bent toward the searchers. I followed it backward easily. I thought I saw a flash of movement near a bush. I swung my light but didn't see anything. Of course not, I chided myself. They already searched this area.

February 1987

Peggy kicked and tried to scream through Daddy's fingers when he dragged her into the car. She even hit him with the little pink plastic purse she carried everywhere. He swore and grabbed a roll of duct tape when she bit him.

I knew it was Daddy because he still drove the same car from when Momma divorced him. I tried to hide, but he saw me and called me over. I stopped far enough away that I could still run if he tried to grab me.

"You didn't see anything, Alanna. Remember that. You didn't see anything. If you say anything I'll kill your sister, and then I'll come back and kill you and your mother. Just remember, bitch, this is all your fault for squealing in the first place."

I saw Peggy's hands scratching at the window as he pulled away, the little beaded bracelet with her name on it rubbing against the fogged up glass. When they found her safe in the forest later that night, she carried no bracelet and no purse. She never asked for either of them again.

02 June 2008, 9:00 pm

Nick Everett met me at the ranger station. He paced with short, jerky steps and wouldn't meet my eyes. I couldn't tell if he was relieved that I was there, or if it made things worse. He held the door of his jeep open for me after moving some pop cans to the side. We started up the access road in silence. Nick shifted his grip five or six times on the steering wheel.

"How long have you been with the Groveton Sheriff's Department?" He shifted his grip again.

"About ten years." Nick knew that. He had been posted to the Mark Twain about half a year before I came back from college. We'd even dated a couple of times.

"How many children's bodies have you found?"

"At least a dozen, but they've always been outsiders. We haven't lost a local child for more than a day in thirty years." I frowned and put my hands on my hips like Granny Eileen used to do. I bumped my elbow on the car door, but he got the idea. "Nick Everett, why are you asking me things you already know?"

He pulled the jeep to the side of the road, parking under a strip of blue material tangled in the trees. "They weren't outsiders, Alanna. Every one of those skeletons belonged to kids that vanished from around here."

I didn't like the direction the conversation took. "They couldn't be. The last one died only a few years ago. The sheriff would have notified the parents, and I would have remembered any little kid that vanished. It would have been in all the newspapers."

Unless a pooka replaced them. Granny Eileen's voice whispered in my head.

Shut up, Granny. You died eight years ago in the mental hospital, raving about my sister.

"They're always older than they look." Nick got out of his jeep and came around to open my door. "Sheriff said you have to help me identify this one so he can close the case."

I knew it would be bad when Nick slipped his fingers through mine and led me through the trees. A stream, swollen with recent rains, crumbled the soil nearby and exposed part of a child's skeleton. Three rangers worked nearby, finishing up the excavation.

Nick handed me a camera. "You're supposed to take pictures."

I snapped the pictures as I mentally catalogued what we found. A child's skeleton, probably female based on the long blonde hair. A piece of duct tape lay in the dirt next to the head. The arms wrapped around a lump of soil. I put the camera down and poked a gloved finger at the lump. The dirt crumbled away to reveal pink plastic. A purse. A child's beaded bracelet circled the wrist. I knew before I looked that the letters would spell out 'PEGGY'

.

March 1990

Leslie Smithy ran away today. She was gone when her mother tried to wake her up for school. The police didn't even search for her. Everyone on Sommers Street heard the argument the night before.

"If you don't like the way we do things in this house, then go ahead and leave, young lady. Maybe it would have been better if you stayed lost."

"Maybe I'll run away and you'll never see me again."

So many teenagers ran away, so many used the same words. Most of the parents didn't even cry. Is it easier to love a lost child than a rebellious teen? A few of us decided to be nicer to our parents: Some of the others just got worse. Everyone thought about running away. Someday I'll run away to the city where they won't tease me about being a country hick like they do at school. I'll go away to college and I'll never come back.

02 June 2008, 11:30 pm

It was Peggy, no doubt about it. I could see the lines on her collar bone from where she fell out of a tree and broke it. The purse and the bracelet just clinched things. The duct tape might still have Daddy's fingerprints on it, but he was long dead in a prison riot. It could only complicate things.

I reeled and fell to my knees. I didn't understand. How could it be Peggy? They found her that night in the forest, found her and brought her home. She grew up with us. Her homecoming picture hung on Momma's living room wall. Homecoming Queen at eighteen, clinging to that football player's arm like she needed an anchor. I can't remember his name. He left to be a big football star at college, but got cut from the team his first year. He never came back. Too embarrassed, I guess. So many high hopes in high school. So many disappointments.

Peggy didn't run away until a month later, when they interviewed that actress.

October 2000

The brand new Groveton Cinema opened yesterday. My sister Peggy cut the ribbon during the ceremony. Everyone in town waited to see "Coal Town Lovers." Not because it ranked well with the critics—it didn't—or starred an important actress—who ever heard of Lee Sommers?—but because we could finally watch a film without traveling forty miles for the privilege. During the first screening, we all got quite a shock.

Mrs. Smithy stood up halfway through the show and screamed, "That's my Leslie!"

A moment later I realized she was right. My one-time best friend made it in Hollywood. I felt proud for her, but a little puzzled. Leslie wanted to.be an actress at five, but forgot all about that after she ran away. She never once acted in a school play or anything before she ran away again at thirteen.

The next day they interviewed the actress on a TV talk show. Lee told the interviewer about running away, and living on the streets for years before she finally got herself in foster care and started up with the school plays. It didn't add up. She didn't have time for all of that to happen to her. Unless she ran away at five.

"She just thinks she's better than all of us, now that she's in Hollywood." I'm not sure who said it first, but everyone agreed. Funny that she chose the name of our street as her new last name.

I thought it was strange that she had some naked scenes in the film. Wasn't she afraid someone would see? Then I realized something: 'Lee' didn't have a little two-inch tail. Instead, two dimpled scars from the ant bites marred her otherwise Hollywood perfect butt. She really wasn't the same girl that ran away at thirteen. Two Leslies.

The next morning Peggy was gone.

03 June 2008, 3:15 am

We've been searching all night for little Mickey. Sheriff Teague told me to take the rest of the night off after I identified Peggy. I just couldn't sit still, so I snuck back against orders. We found my sister. At least we thought we did. But little Mickey is still out there somewhere. Most of the searchers are dropping out, and a few people are starting to wonder aloud if we'll actually find him.

Me, I'm starting to wonder if we've run out of pookas. The fairies didn't take Leslie, and they didn't take Peggy. They just replaced them. So many people joke about Granny Eileen's madness, but I believe her pookas are real. We'll find Mickey—or a changeling that looks just like him, at least—if we concentrate on searching long enough. I just wish I could concentrate; I keep seeing my sister Peggy in my thoughts.

Nick Everett tells me they'll bury her in the cemetery for unclaimed children. I wish they could tell Momma about Peggy's body being found. I understand why the Sheriff and the Rangers don't say anything, though. What happens when people learn about the pookas? Will they stop believing that the children will be found? Will we be like every other town that locks their doors all day and locks their children up like they're in prison? Will we grieve for our lost little ones?

If only I could find Peggy... wait, we're looking for Mickey. I have to concentrate. I'll probably wonder for the rest of my life why the pookas replace the little ones but never the teenagers. Do parents love their little children better than their teens? Or is it just easier to let go of an older child? Do the fairies want our grief like Granny Eileen said? Or are they trying to heal it?

A shout goes up nearby. "I've found tracks!"

The few searchers left are converging around us. I go a few steps further and see a foot sticking out beneath a bush. I sing out, "I've found someone!"

We push the bushes aside and I bring my flashlight up. The light wavers and falls as my hand goes numb.

There is a child hiding beneath the bushes. It's a pooka child. There is no question about it. I understand now why Sheriff Teague told me to go home. I should never have come back here. It's too late.

Another light shines under the bush. The child clings to the bush and raises his right hand to block the light. It's Mickey O'Neill's red hair I see sticking from behind the branches. His eye sparkles, as green as an emerald. His freckles practically glow in the dark.

Someone reaches down to pull him out, and everyone gasps. The other side—the left side of his face--is as unspotted as milk. Peggy's long blonde hair frames half of her heart-shaped face, staring from a frightened, blue eye as she realizes something is badly wrong.

Granny Eileen was right. The pookas will break everyone's hearts. If we don't do it first.

The Mermaid

A trading ship just come from round old Cathay
Heard a noise as it tucked past a rock in the bay.
A voice, very female, drifted in from the waves:
A beautiful voice, with overtones of watery graves.

"Mermaid!" "Siren!" "Seawitch!" They cried.
Some few (not too bright) jumped in over the side.
One shark-bit, five drowned, one whose lungs had quite
burst,
Were pulled back aboard, along with one who cursed,
"I wanted to see her!" He cried with a shout.
His voice cried from the brig, "Let me out! Let me out!"
The captain ignored him, focused on his course,
Prayed silently for an easier threat—like the Norse.

The mermaid wailed, wished she knew the words
To say, "I give warning! Look up at the birds!"
For the seabirds avoided a large patch of sea
Where in no time at all the trading ship would be.
A sea serpent, she knew, soon surfaced to feed,
And the ship, in its jaws, would snap like a reed.
"Why won't they understand?" She asked in her wail.
The ship, for more speed, put up fore and aft sail.

The sea churned wildly ahead of the ship.
The captain screamed, "Lifeboats!" as he fell on his hip.
The serpent approached; he prepared himself to die.
His attention was captured by the mermaid's wailing cry.
With a last glance at his ship, he leaped over the side.
A nearby dolphin took him for a ride.

Colleen H. Robbins

The serpent ate his ship, then finished off the crew,
He told himself sternly, "That could have been you."

The mermaid sighed with relief—she'd saved one.
In past times that number had often been none.
She directed the dolphin to take him to shore,
And resolved to herself that she'd find him once more.

My Courtesan

My courtesan, oh lovely one,
An angel you have been borne.
Do you ever run under the sun
And hear the faint hunting horn?

Did you learn your skill upon a hill
And practiced 'til you did well?
Do you still (or perhaps you will)
Change at what price you sell?

The money you made as you plied your trade
Does it support a child?
Do your children wade or play in the shade
Or just run a bit more wild?

The nobles bet that all your "get"
Will soon be caught as thieves.
Resist that bet or will you let
Them be beggars and such as these?

Oh courtesan, oh lovely one,
I'm pining for love of you.
You are such fun, but still I run,
For marry you I'll not do.

Colleen H. Robbins

Arena!

Circular tiers about the sand;
The Emperor comes and all do stand.
Warriors hold hands to the sky.
Saluting while they wonder why.

Contests begin at Emperor's smile,
And men are dying all the while.
The winners halt and try to mend,
For fighting here's far from its end.

The beast comes in and stalks across
The burning sands. A knife is tossed.
A beast will fall and men as well;
Caligula laughs at new-made hell.

Stormy

Serah bounced in place at the bus stop, pink kitty backpack at her feet. When the bus pulled up, she ran up the steps and plopped into the seat next to a girl with long brown hair. "Hi, Jasmine! How was your summer?"

Jasmine leaned up close to Serah and whispered in her ear. "Star had five kittens. They're almost big enough to give away. Can you come over after school and see them?"

After school, the kittens were all snuggled up to Star, drinking their milk. Serah counted them. Two black kittens, two white kittens with black spots, one orange and white kitten, and a larger gray kitten with ruffled fur on the sides.

"There are six kittens! I like the big gray one. It looks like a storm cloud," Serah said.

"What gray one?" asked Jasmine.

Serah carefully petted the gray kitten with one finger. "This one," she said.

The kitten purred and backed away from Star, then nuzzled Serah's finger and spread its wings.

"What is that?" Jasmine pointed her finger at the gray kitten as it flapped its wings.

"Cool!" exclaimed Serah. "A flying kitty!"

The kitten circled around Serah's head, then flew right out Jasmine's window. Jasmine jumped up and closed the window. Serah ran outside.

She looked up in the trees and down under the bushes, but Serah could not find the flying kitten. After an hour, she had to go home.

Serah ran right into her room and flopped on the bed. She worried about the flying gray kitten.

Scratch! Scratch! The noise came from the window.

There on the windowsill sat the flying kitten. Serah opened her window. The kitten flew right down to her bed and curled up on the pillow.

"Serah, time for dinner," called her Mom.

"You be a good kitty," Serah warned. "I'll bring you some milk after dinner."

After eating, Serah went back to her room and closed the door behind her. What a mess! Pencils rolled on the floor, her favorite green crayon was chewed in half, and two shredded Pokemon cards peeked out from under the bed. The gray kitten sat on top of the bookshelf, licking its tail.

Knock. Knock. "Serah, open your door. It's Mom."

Serah opened her door a tiny crack. "What?"

Mom pushed her way into the room. "What are you up to in here?" Mom looked around at the mess.

The flying kitten swooped down and almost hit Mom in the nose. It tipped to one side and flew out into the hallway.

"What was that?" asked Mom.

"It is one of Jasmine's kittens," said Serah.

"Then it is going back to Jasmine's house. We can't have a kitten flying around loose."

Mom called Jasmine's mother. "We need to bring back your kitten."

"We still have all five kittens," said Jasmine's mother.

'The gray one that flies. You have to take it back," Mom insisted.

"A flying kitten? No, that one wasn't one of ours."

Mom hung up the phone, and then untangled the kitten from the window curtain. She handed the flying kitten to Serah. "You think of a name for him, and I'll be right back."

When Mom returned with a large birdcage a few minutes later, Serah carefully wrote the perfect name on a card: Stormy.

Night Breeze

I cannot forget the leap of the leopard,
The blood on its spots as it died at my feet.
The time seemed forever as I limped a'homeward,
My knife dripping blood in my bowl of flour'd wheat.

And the dream still goes on--the scent of my prey
Sings hot on the night breeze as I run away.
And the kill will be swift when the hunt is all done,
For I am the huntress, and still, I run.

The slash in my leg that mixes our blood
As scarlet drops spatter upon golden hide.
It healed fast, though not clean, smeared with black mud,
And now my own horses will not let me ride.

And the dream still goes on--the scent of my prey
Sings hot on the night breeze as I run away.
And the kill will be swift when the hunt is all done,
For I am the huntress, and still, I run.

They say that a lion or similar beast
Has come to the area, killed all the sheep.
And a half-dozen hunters sought to stop its cruel feast
Became six more victims, left untouched in a heap.

And the dream still goes on--the scent of my prey
Sings hot on the night breeze as I run away.
And the kill will be swift when the hunt is all done,
For I am the huntress, and still, I run.

Yet I know of those hunters. I saw them one night
Their faces illumined by moonlight, I think.
They hunted for me, which didn't seem right
For my head was bent at the stream where I drink.

Colleen H. Robbins

And the dream still goes on--the scent of my prey
Sings hot on the night breeze as I run away.
And the kill will be swift when the hunt is all done,
For I am the huntress, and still, I run.

The dreams are much clearer now—I see those I know,
Though I feel myself hidden well within trees.
Soon my hunt will be over, my long hunt, and so
I feel I must prepare to soon leave.

And the dream still goes on—the scent of my prey
Sings hot on the night breeze as I run away.
And the kill will be swift when the hunt is all done,
For I am the huntress, and still, I run.

The stalking is finished. A swift final leap
To land on my victim--I know that I will
As I break glass and land in the house where I sleep,
For it is my own self that I must now kill.

And the dream still goes on--the scent of my prey
Sings hot on the night breeze as I run away.
And the kill will be swift when the hunt is all done,
For I am the huntress, and still, I run.

And it is no dream, the leopard's revenge,
For outside I see now the light of the sun.
Its own death the leopard has truly avenged,
For now I'm the leopard—and still, I run.

Gerald's Gargoyle

The evidence is fleeting:
A shadow against the moon,
A muddy footprint on a railroad tie,
The hunter blasting his gun
Into the night.

Is it wounded?
A trail of fine sand
suggests so.

Noisy elephants at the zoo
loyally protect their young
and take on the task
of protecting its pile of ovoid rocks
that it left in their yard.

But with Gerald's gargoyle gone,
how can its eggs ever hatch?

Colleen H. Robbins

The Last Unicorn

The moonbeams slice through darkest night;
A fair young maid doth weep.
A clatter low upon the road,
It makes her heart to leap.

Of silver, gold, and legends told,
The unicorn stands tall,
His search, they say, by moonlit way:
The purest heart of all.

Her tears have dried; she mounts the side
Of Unicorn's last son.
And moonbeams twirl about the girl
As into the sky they run.

Barbarian

The cold winds blow, predicting snow,
And all look up the hill.
A man stands there without a care,
Shouldering he his kill.

This fur-clad man, from him they ran,
For civilized men were they.
"Barbarian!" They cry and run,
For fighting is not their way.

His kill he lays upon the graves
Performing a simple chant,
The soul to rest among the best,
King's honours he does so grant.

A war breaks out, a total rout
Of enemies to the "good"—
They kill again, those civilized men
Forgotten dead left in the wood.

A lone man sighs as winds of ice
Whistle around his head.
Barbarian, honourable man,
He never forgets his dead.

Author's Note:
ME MERRY WIFE was originally written as a radio play.
Angus and Robbie are sailors, old and young, and are
shipmates.

ME MERRY WIFE

SCENE 1.

(FOOTSTEPS. CHAIR SCRAPE. GLASSES CLINK.)

BARMAID: What'll it be, sailor?

ANGUS: Rum. Just rum, Lass.

(GLASSES CLINK. POURING LIQUID.)

BARMAID: Here you go.

(FOOTSTEPS APPROACH. COINS CLINK.)

ANGUS: That's a good lass.

BARMAID: (GIGGLES)

ROBBIE: Uh uh, Angus. Flirting with this fine young
thing. What about your wife?

ANGUS: Aye, me merry wife. Seven long years I've
spent on ships, working to make me fortune so we can finally
have the child she wants so badly. The last ship got delayed

42

a week by a storm. She always greets me so well! But this time I come home with a chest full of gold, and I find out she's left me for another man. (PAUSE) Now I've got to go find him, Robbie. Find him before there's trouble.

(GULPING. GLASS SLAMMED ON WOOD)

ROBBIE: You don't mean to kill him?

ANGUS: No, I mean to warn him. (LOUDER) Lass, another.

SCENE 2

(FOGHORN. WATER SLAPPING AGAINST SHIPS. RATTLE OF ROPES AND CABLES, FLAPPING SAILS, FOGHORN.)

SAILOR #1: (OFF) Coming about.

CAPTAIN: (OFF) Hard a lee

SAILOR #1: Captain, there's a ship ahead. I don't see anyone moving on deck. She looks like she's adrift.

CAPTAIN: Angus, choose a small crew and take a dory across. If she's abandoned, I'm claiming salvage.

ANGUS: Yes, Sir!

(LOUD SPLASH. FOOTSTEPS ON WOOD. RHYTHMIC SPLASH OF ROWING, CREAKING ROPES. WATER SPLASHING)

ANGUS: Hello the ship. Request permission to come aboard. Hello? (PAUSE) (LOW) I don't think anyone is there.

(LOUDER) We're coming aboard to assist you.

(CLATTERING WOOD.)

ANGUS: Robbie, don't come up here

ROBBIE: Why not? I (PAUSE) Oh my God.
(VOMITING NOISES.)

SAILOR #1   (LOW) So much blood.

ROBBIE: What could do such a thing? They're all torn
apart.

ANGUS: I've seen two like this before. Every seven
years it happens. I'm sure we'll hear of others when we
reach our next port. Let's get her cleaned up enough to
salvage.

SCENE 3.

(TELEGRAPH /RADIO TOWER NOISE)

RADIO ANNOUNCER: (D) This is a breaking news alert. A
fourth cargo ship with the entire crew massacred has been
recovered off the New England Coast. Ships logs indicate a
small line of squalls as the last entry. A series of similar
attacks occurred in the same area just seven years ago.

(TELEGRAPH/RADIO TOWER NOISE)

SCENE 4.

44

(MUSIC: SAILOR'S BAR AMBIENCE OR "DRUNKEN SAILOR." CLINKING GLASSES.)

ROBBIE: That salvaged ship earned us a pretty penny.

ANGUS: Aye, it did, Robbie. But that's no comfort to the families of the dead.

ROBBIE: Do you think they hooked a shark and it got loose on deck?

ANGUS: No, that was no shark attack. Let's talk about something more pleasant.

ROBBIE: What about Meredith? How did you meet?

ANGUS: Meredith? Oh, me merry wife. She's not named Meredith. I just call her Merry.

ROBBIE: Do you have a picture of her? You've spoken of her so often over the years, but I've never seen her.

ANGUS: A picture. (LAUGHS) I've kept a picture of her these last seven years. She was from the South Seas, you know. A little island where we pulled in for fresh water. I met her on the shore. She looked like one of them Tahiti girls: sun brown skin, wide cheekbones, long dark hair her only clothing. I remember thinking that she must have just finished swimming because of the seaweed caught in her hair. We carried a group of newsmen on that trip, men with more money than sense. One took a picture of me Merry. She screeched like a seagull in her home tongue. One of my shipmates spoke pidgin, made enough sense of her foreign words to tell me why she was terrified. The picture had "stolen her skin," she said, and she couldn't go home. So, I bought the picture and took care of her. She has the sweetest voice when she's calm.

ROBBIE: Why couldn't she go home?

ANGUS: I never figured that out. She wouldn't talk about it even after I civilized her. She made me swear to never show the picture to anyone. I didn't, either, until the worst of the storm last week when I took it out to say goodbye to her. A wave plucked the photograph right out of my hand and swirled it right to the Bosun's feet. He leaned over, picked it up, and stared right at it. I snatched it back and tried to dry it, but the picture faded. It's nothing but a stained piece of paper, now.

(RATTLE OF PAPER)

ROBBIE: This used to be a photograph? Why do you keep it?

ANGUS: I still remember what she looked like. I don't need to see it with me eyes. We'd better get back to the ship.

ROBBIE: Maybe I'll meet a Tahiti girl of my own someday.

ANGUS: I hope not, for your sake.

SCENE 5

(FOGHORN, WATER SLAPPING AGAINST WOODEN SHIPS, ROPES AND CABLES RATTLING, FLAPPING

SAILS, FOGHORN.)

ROBBIE: Angus, you've got to give up on this vendetta. You've asked about Merry and her companion at every port of call. I'm sure they've already gotten word. Besides, the massacres are happening more frequently. We've salvaged six ships, and there's at least a dozen others that we've heard of. I'm thinking about staying at the next port. I want to live.

ANGUS: I don't think they've heard. There have only been six ships that left any of our ports of call before we did, and we've pulled all six in for salvage.

(RISING WIND)

ROBBIE: It's like we're cursed.

ANGUS: No, Robbie. I think we've been blessed so far, but I don't think it's going to last. At the last two ports I described me Merry, but I also described you.

ROBBIE: Me? Why would you do that?

ANGUS: I wanted to check if you'd been asking about her. After a while I noticed that you'd already been to each pub before I got there. Last port, you did the same. Problem was, you kept forgetting to mention she was me wife. I think maybe you've already found your Tahiti girl, 'cept for one thing. Me Merry doesn't come from Tahiti. She's from an older place.

SAILOR #1:   (OFF) Squalls approaching, Captain.

CAPTAIN: (OFF) Batten down the hatches!

(HIGH WINDS. LOUD SPLASHES. RIPPING SAILS)

SAILOR #1:   We're taking on water!

ROBBIE: What are those lights? Is that Saint Elmo's fire?

SAILOR #1:   Devil Fire! Abandon Ship!

(FOUR LOUD SPLASHES)

ANGUS: Saint Elmo's fire means the ship won't sink.

                   I'm not saying we'll survive,

but we'll be seeing me merry wife soon

ROBBIE: You mean she's dead?

ANGUS: No. She's over there with her sisters.

(WIND AND WAVE SOUNDS FADE. THREE SMALL SPLASHES. MUSIC: "MY BONNY LIES OVER THE OCEAN." FIRST HALF-VERSE PIPED.)

ROBBIE: What? Who is that? Meredith?

MERRY: Robbie, you left me behind when you promised you'd take me.

ROBBIE: I had to. Angus was with me.

ANGUS: I never left you behind, me Merry. I brought you home a chest of gold, just as I promised. Now we can have those children you've been dreaming about.

MERRY: Angus, me Angus. You were so late I thought you forgot your promises.

ANGUS: Never. I'd never forget your mating season.

ROBBIE: (LOW) Mating season?

MERRY: We nearly missed it. My sisters have all mated, and they're so hungry now.

ANGUS: I've saved me best parts for you.

ROBBIE: Meredith, no! You can have my best parts.

(LOUD SPLASH. SWIMMING NOISES.)

ANGUS: Robbie, you're a fool. Merry isn't short for Meredith.

MERRY: It's short for Merrow, and I always enjoy a good pre-mating meal.

SCENE 6.

(FOGHORN, WATER SLAPPING WOOD, RATTLE OF METAL PIECES, FLAPPING SAILS, FOGHORN.)

SAILOR # 2: Is there anyone alive down there?

ANGUS: Aye. Me merry wife and I. I think the others are all dead.

SAILOR #2:   Here, I'll help your wife, and (PAUSE) Oh Lord!

ANGUS: I've been shark-bit, but me Merry is a nurse of sorts. She used my belt to save the rest of the leg. Do you have any food? We've been out here since the squall swamped us nearly two weeks ago. I could stand to lose some weight, but I'm worried about my wife. She's newly pregnant, and twins run in her family.

END

Midnight Visitor

A whisper of wings—the faintest of neighs—
Ah! The falconer returns early one day
From hunting—but no, for I hear not the sound
Of hooves upon dank and marshy ground.

A robber perhaps, while our lord is away?
He returns so soon—the dawn's very day.
CREAK—could that be the barn door opening?
The horses seem quiet... What is this thing?

Carefully, carefully—make not a sound
As we unbolt the shutter, peer in and around...
What's this? A wing-tip of silvery white?
But the size of that wing! This can't be right.

The barn door flies open—a horse prances forth.
A horse?—no, a Pegasus—turns to the North.
Wings snap; a white feather falls to the ground
As our visitor leaves: the only trace 'twill be found.

Colleen H. Robbins

The Dragon's Quest

Author's note: This poem is based entirely on heraldry [the pictures often found on flags and shields]. "Atlantean East" refers to the East Coast of the US (on the Atlantic Ocean), "Nottinghill Coill Barony" covered much of South Carolina, and "Tear's Sea Shore Canton" refers specifically to Charleston, SC [In the naming conventions of the SCA]. The symbol of Tear's Sea Shore was an ocean wave breaking into froth at the top.

The "Order of the Shore's Defenders" was a newly created award for SCA fighters who lived in or near Charleston and had placed well in large tournaments. At the time this poem was written, there were only two members. One's shield had a salamander (fire spirit) and the other's shield had an eye painted on it.

The Dragon's Quest

A she-dragon watching her eggs start to hatch
Thought, "My young will be hungry; I'll get them a batch
Of maidens to eat and a few children, too.
Now where do I get them?" She thought she knew.

She'd heard of a Barony new to the East;
Nottinghill Coill would provide quite a feast.
They had yet no Champions, if she'd heard aright.
They would be easy pickings—no one to fight.

And Tear Sea's Shore Canton, so far from the rest
(A messenger to the Baron would take two days at best)
"They'd be a good start," she said with a smirk,

And flew on to the Shore to begin her sweet work.

On arriving she drew to the sky with surprise.
The populace awaited her by the seaside.
Their bravery had her quite taken aback
When two fighters strode forth to meet her attack.

A dragon flames hot, but the Salamander's worse.
She quickly drew up to fly full in reverse.
Hiding in clouds, she attempted to flee,
But the Eye saw her hide and told where she would be.

She hadn't expected to find such contenders:
The entire Order of the Shore's Defenders,
Who suddenly backed up, eyes to the sky.
She started to worry, not knowing quite why.

"A fast-coming roar," her ears said, "is behind."
She did not want to look, afraid of what she'd find.
More afraid not to see what sounded atop her,
She looked up, saw an ocean wave breaking (proper).

The dragon (half-drowned) left Tear Sea's Shore with haste.
"I'll get my revenge; I'll lay the Coill to waste."
She flew on to the West, prepared to spit flame,
Then quickly flew home, her skin red-tinged with shame:

For even a dragon can sometimes forget
What happens to fire when it gets a bit wet.
Some years later her young asked where they should feast.
She replied, "The Knowne World... but not the Atlantean
East!"

Pheasantus Phoenicius

Brittany walked through the lab's animal room like a tourist, gaping at the array of strange birds caged inside. Between the bower birds and the others stood a cage of ring-necked pheasants, a bird she was certain was not native to Papua New Guinea. One last cage stood by itself in the far corner.

The last bird was unfamiliar to her. Granted, it was her first trip, but she spent months studying every published article, video, and photograph of the island's unique bird population. The specimen stalked around its cage like it owned the room, bobbing its head up and down on a long loon-like neck. Brittany bent closer. The coloring superficially resembled the ring-necked pheasants she knew from her youth, white ring around the neck and red-brown speckled flight feathers laying lengthwise along the wings and tail. It turned its head and she jerked back. The beak's swollen base flattened into a triangular duck-like bill scaled along half its length. This was no pheasant.

With a two-note cry reminiscent of a peacock, the bird spread its wings and lunged forward. Short purplish-red feathers stood erect among the brown as a six-inch tongue of flame erupted from the bird's chest. She scrambled backward, bumping into a lab tech.

The tech lifted her to her feet. "I see you've met Sparky." He chuckled and stuck out a hand patched with shiny burn scars. "Douglas Jackson."

"Brittany Kay. Thanks for the help."

"Sparky's not usually so aggressive. You must have startled him. C'mon, let's get you a white suit and I'll show you the Clean Room. Welcome to the project."

\#

Brittany tucked a trailing red curl up under her white cap before examining Sparky. Her gene splicing and cloning techniques worked best with the nucleus inserted into the egg of a similar bird. Sparky pecked at a bit of wild grain on her hand, wings braced against the bars of his cage.

"Careful there. He bit the last tech to get that close, and then fried her." Doug came around the corner carrying a water jug.

"I'm not afraid of a pinch."

"No, really. He bit her. That beak of his has some sharp teeth, hooked backward like a snake. Tore the crap out of Suzanne's hand."

"I haven't met Suzanne yet."

"You won't. She left the project." He moved back among the cages, refilling water bottles and bowls.

Sparky pushed his beak into her empty hand, scratching at the bars of his cage. Brittany frowned. The bird's scaly feet were planted firmly on the floor of the cage.

"Sorry Sparky, all done for today."

Sparky stretched his long neck toward her retreating hand, rubbing his mid-wing joints along the bars. A purple feather dislodged and floated down to the lab floor. Something white flashed from between the feathers and back before she could focus on it.

"Doug, did you see that?"

"Guess not. Let's check the video room. Sparky's under constant surveillance."

She followed Doug through the door in the back into the pristine hallway. They ignored the door that led to the changing areas and Clean room, passed by the examination rooms, and entered a small office cluttered with computers and monitors. It took Doug only a moment to bring up three views of Sparky side-by-side, each labeled and time-stamped.

"Rewind until just before his feather fell."

"He dropped a feather?" Doug left her in front of the monitors as he dashed back out. A few minutes later he came back in, brandishing a long pair of forceps with the feather clasped between.

"Two years, Brit. Two years and this is the first feather we've gotten from any of them." He thrust a specimen bottle in her direction. "Unscrew this, please."

Brittany held the open bottle out as Doug dropped the feather in. "Sparky's not the only one?"

Doug didn't answer. Up on the screen Sparky stretched out his neck to follow her hand and pushed his wings against the bars.

"Slow it down. Watch his wing joints." She pointed at the monitor as the image slowed. "There." She stared at the image on the screen, blinking only when Doug enlarged the best image. A printer hummed somewhere in the room as Brittany tried to catch her breath. Three claws peeked out from between the feathers, well defined against the bars. She put her hand up against the screen, fingers splayed. "Three grasping claws, and a finger bone extending into the outer wing. There's a claw tip showing from the other wing, too. I can't tell if Sparky is an archaeopteryx or related to those feathered dinosaurs from China. I need to see an x-ray."

"We don't have any x-rays."

"Well, what about blood tests?"

"None of those, either. The birds die when we try."

"What about a necropsy report. Surely you have one of those."

"Brit, I can't answer your questions. You need to talk to Director Hanse when he gets back next week."

#

"I don't understand why you haven't x-rayed Sparky yet. We need some sort of scans. So far all I know about is a single feather, and the photograph of his wing claws."

"Sparky? Oh, you mean specimen PP-06. What feather? What photograph? We have no such evidence. Doug would have called me right away if anything important happened." Hanse smiled, reminding her of a shady used

56

car salesman. "Perhaps you dreamed. There are plenty of potent flowers growing around here. It wouldn't be the first time someone hallucinated. The girl you replaced, for example. She had a Bunsen burner accident, and tried to blame it on a specimen." He chuckled, the strained sound unconvincing.

"Just check the surveillance tapes." Brittany took a deep breath, trying to calm herself.

"The tapes overwrite themselves every other day. Even if there had been something, it is long gone by now." He tapped his pen on the desk a few times. "If there is nothing else, I for one have work to do."

She stood up and headed for the office door. As she turned the knob, she stopped.

"Remember, no x-rays or scans of the specimen. If it dies, you are terminated."

#

Three weeks later, Sparky dropped another feather. She grabbed a glove, picked up the feather, and peeled the glove inside out around her prize. Sparky showed his claws again, so she waited until Doug headed for the bathroom and printed her own pictures. Five prints hummed out of the printer, to be folded and slid inside the waistband of her pants. She was printing a sixth when Doug came in.

"What are you doing?"

"Sparky showed his claws again. See?" She held out the picture.

Doug snatched it away. "I'll bring it to the Director." He marched out.

The next morning, the back room was locked for the first time since Brittany started working there. When it opened again two days later, she queued up a picture of an archaeopteryx skeleton, focusing on the wing claws.

"Hey Doug, can I see that photograph I gave you? I want to compare the claws."

"Photograph? What are you talking about?" Doug peered over her shoulder. "Stop surfing the web and get back to work."

That same afternoon, Ben, the other tech, returned from a collecting trip. He opened his bag and produced four purple-speckled brown eggs, slightly larger than chicken eggs. "Let's get them in the incubator."

After she safely stowed the eggs, Brittany helped Ben set up four more cages around the room.

"What kind of eggs are these? And how do you know what temperature to put them in?"

"Pheasantus phoenicius. They seem so similar to pheasants that we have been incubating them about ten degrees higher than their norm. I just hope we hatch a female this time. So far everything has been males. We have to keep the males separated because they fight. We lost Bic and Butane that way."

"Earlier specimens?" Brittany asked. Doug had already implied this, but would not answer any direct questions.

"Five of them. Here, let me show you their files." Ben took her to a side room, with overstuffed file drawers. He dug around in one for a moment, and came up with a handful of nearly empty folders.

There were no x-rays of Sparky or the other five specimens labeled "Pheasantus phoenicius." No x-rays, no blood tests, and no necropsy reports. Just a simple notation in the other charts: deceased and cremated.

Ben made up four new charts, labeling them with numbers PP007 through PP010. He added a single line to each. "Collected as eggs from the side of Mount Giluwe, approximate height of nest: 4300 meters.

"That seems awfully high up."

"Yeah, I rescued these eggs from the path of a lava flow. The female is as dumb as a dodo. She keeps leaving little nests all over the volcano, and so many of her eggs get incinerated."

"Where were the others collected?" Brit closed the files.

"Same circumstances, different volcano. The Director empties their files after they die."

#

The following week, Ben poked his head into the main room. "I'm headed into town to buy supplies. Want to ride along?"

Brittany scrambled to get her carry-all. Nearly three hours later the boat docked at another island. As she walked down the dock, the colorful clothes of the people and their many blankets and booths with local crafts made her think of the tourist-stops she and her friend Amanda made on their way to and from the Galapagos Islands to study sea turtles and land tortoises. Burying temperature sensors in the top and bottom of the nests to correlate temperatures with the sexes of the various terrapins was important work to keep the species from going extinct. It was, however, boring, and their twice a month trips to the touristy areas kept them excited.

"Hey, Brit, there's a larger marketplace close to the Post Office. Follow me."

She dutifully followed Ben as he entered a small building and came out with a sackful of mail. "We keep a Post Office box here. I'll give you the address in case you want to write home."

"That would be great."

Ben pointed down the street. "I'm going down there to buy fruit and what groceries I can find. Why don't you look at the shops?"

Brittany wandered around, absolutely fascinated with the amount of carvings—particularly turtles and birds—that she found. Next time she would have to buy a gift for Amanda.

Ben returned before long, followed by several men carrying crates. "Back to the boat."

By the time the boat pulled in near their research facility, the sun hung low in the sky. After offloading the crates, Brittany made a final check of her subjects and then collapsed in her room. She wrote a long letter to Amanda telling her about the beauty of Papua New Guinea, then added a few questions about her friend's current research among the turtles.

#

She collected two more feathers from Sparky over the next two weeks. One vanished into Doug's care, followed by a lecture on caring for Sparky. The bird had never shed so many feathers before and must be feeling ill.

So many feathers, she thought. *Amazing how the feathers you tried to gaslight me about are suddenly real again.*

When Ben's next supply run came due, Doug assigned her extra work. She handed Ben her letter and asked him to mail it for her.

"Sure thing!" He waved to her as he set off in the boat.

Two supply runs later, he brought her a return letter. Brittany read it that evening.

Amanda received a promotion, and they secured a new grant. She could now run bits of shell samples for DNA on the turtles. She was very excited, and also met a new research assistant just a few years older. "A match made in Turtledom," she declared.

Brittany laughed at that, and smiled at the postscript scrawled across the end of the letter. "PS. I would LOVE a turtle craft from your supply town. Keep it small, though. I can only fit about six more inches of turtles on my shelf. Love, Amanda."

#

Brittany's return letter to Amanda mentioned how sweet Ben was, and how difficult Doug could be. "It almost seems as if he is conspiring with Director Hanse to get rid of me. I'm tired of his lies, too. Anything I give to him for the director seems to vanish into thin air." She left the handwritten letter in her notebook.

They finally allowed her to accompany Ben on short trips up the volcano, looking for eggs. Ben pointed out one nest, more a pile of rocks barely surrounding the eggs. It sat too close to the lava flow to save, and the eggs were lost, disappearing under dark red lava. Brittany marveled how the coldest birds on the planet built nests so much like those of the hottest: penguins and phoenix birds.

Brittany found the next nest. This one held six eggs. She carefully packed them in her insulated carryall, using a heat-resistant scoop to nestle them into the asbestos padding. She added an extra layer of insulation on one end, the eggs hot enough to melt it around the edges.

Ben also found a nest that they barely saved, containing four eggs. After he packed down his eggs, they headed back down the volcano and headed for the facility. They arrived just past lunchtime.

She managed to get out on the supply run the next day, finding a little box that looked like a sea turtle floating on the ocean, just the right size for Amanda's shelf. She brought it back to the station and left it on the nightstand, safe in its unmarked box. She did not mention who it was for, nor did she tell anyone about the secret compartment between the turtle's ocean and the base of the sculpture.

Later that afternoon, while visiting Sparky, Doug approached her.

"You'd best watch out for Ben. He's not who you think he is."

"What do you mean? Who do you think I think he is?" *What an odd comment*, Brittany thought.

"He's not boyfriend material, no matter what your friend from turtle research says. You shouldn't get entangled with the other employees."

"What? Have you been reading my mail?" She curled her lip into a sneer. "That's a breach of privacy."

"I have to make sure that you're not telling anyone about our research." Doug tilted his head back, nose prominently in the air.

"We study birds, Doug. It's not like we're developing weapons or anything."

Doug's eyes widened, pupils expanding fully for a moment before he dashed from the room.

Ben came in an hour later. "Hey, Brit. Are you sending that sea turtle to Amanda? I've got the perfect box for it. We can make an extra run tomorrow for you to send it off."

Brittany felt trapped. Ben knew the content of her letters, too? "Sure, sounds good." She finished up and went back to her room.

She wrote a quick note to Amanda, asking her for a DNA analysis of the feather and warning her that Doug read the mail. "Please wait for another letter with a different address before sending the results of the DNA analysis. Think Archy." She tucked the note and one photograph of Sparky's wing claws in with one of Sparky's feathers, still encased in the inside-out glove, and slid it into the secret compartment, then hurriedly closed it and put it back in the original box.

After dinner, she went to see Ben and repackage the sculpture.

He carefully opened the box and checked the packing material, the packed it back together. He pulled out a slightly larger box.

They really are looking for hidden items, she thought. "Wait--let me just write a quick note on it." She took a pen and leaned over.

"To my favorite turtle girl. Don't let it eat plastic! -Brit"

"Plastic?" Ben tilted his head and looked into her eyes.

"Plastic," she affirmed. "It's an inside joke."

"Explain it to me, please." His voice sounded tense.

"Amanda always complained during necropsies that the turtles ate more plastic than jellyfish. So every time we had jelly, or saw a toy turtle, we'd joke about plastic."

"Oh. I meant to ask you, where did you put your egg carryall? I wanted to log in and number the eggs."

"In the front end of the incubator. Isn't it there?"

"I didn't see it."

The two went back in the room with the incubator, searching for the missing carryall. Twenty minutes later, they found it in the refrigerator.

"Oh, Brit. I don't know who would have done this. Six eggs, gone like that." Ben snapped his fingers.

Doug came into the room. "I see you found the missing eggs. Very careless of you."

Brittany looked at him through slitted eyes. *She had her suspicions, all right.* "Well, if they're dead, than may I keep one in my room?"

"You won't be able to take it with you when you go."

"I know. They're just so beautiful."

"I suppose."

Brittany opened the box. The eggs looked intact, and actually felt warm. They hadn't been in the refrigerator for long. She chose an egg from the end with extra padding, where the insulation partially melted across the eggs, and took it with her.

That night she slipped into the lab room and took out a Bunsen burner. She had a theory to test, a theory that she tested before with the turtles. Higher temperatures produced more females with turtles, so why wouldn't it work with a bird whose eggs were always found near volcanic vents and lava flows?

She hooked the Bunsen burner up to the gas vent in the corner of the older lab. The burner lit. She put the egg in a metal cradle and set it above the burner, then turned the heat up as far as it would go. *1500 degrees Celsius, that's 2700 degrees Fahrenheit*, she mentally calculated. *I wonder if it's hot enough?*

#

The next morning she was ready to go. She carried her precious package as Ben drove the boat for supplies. They stopped first at the post office and mailed her package. The postmaster—the only postal worker—promised it would go out on the afternoon boat. From there, he explained, it might take a month or two to get to its destination.

"Now that I've mailed a souvenir to Amanda, I'll find one for myself. Want to help?"

Ben pulled his hands up to his chest and showed her his palms. "No, thanks. I've got supplies to buy. Have fun." He walked on down the street.

Once Ben was out of sight, she bought herself a painted carving of a Bird of Paradise, the symbol on the flag of Papua New Guinea. This particular bird was painted in shades of magenta and red. She returned to the post office and bought a mailing box.

The postmaster came over. "Anything I do help?"

She pointed at the boxes where people got their mail. "I want to rent one of these, have my own address that no one knows but me."

"Ah, boyfriend. Good job. I let you have this one and no give them you mail." They bargained for a price which Brittany thought quite reasonable, but was probably too high based on the gleeful look on the postmaster's face. She bought some paper and an envelope and dashed off a quick note to Amanda with the new address.

#

She managed to keep the Bunsen burner going for almost two weeks before the gas ran out. They traced the "leak" to the old lab, and found her egg.

Doug rounded on her. "What did you think you were doing?"

"Testing a theory that the eggs that died from cold were not really dead." Brittany grabbed the Bunsen burner, dialing it all the way down. "Someone messed with my settings, though. I have no idea what temperature it was heated at."

Doug glanced at the now cooling egg. "Well, it's still dead." He looked back at her. "You wasted resources that we needed. Director Hanse will be quite angry."

Brittany stared. Did the egg just move? *It did*!

"Well, what do you have to say for yourself?" Doug tapped a foot on the floor, the noise nearly covering the sounds from the egg.

"It's hatching." She barely got the words out.

"What was that? A smart remark? You'll be out of here soon. "

"I said the egg is hatching."

"Funny." The egg made noise behind him. Doug whirled around. "It's hatching!" He bobbed up and down. "What are you waiting for? Get it a cage in the warming room."

#

The chick looked drab and brown, similar to the pheasant chicks they occasionally hatched. Ben took notes, including the number of hours the egg had been refrigerated.

"Are you certain the heat was set on 150 degrees? Is that Celsius or Fahrenheit?"

"I set it on 150 degrees Celsius late last night," Brittany said. "I woke up with the idea to try and hatch it. I don't remember looking at the clock, so I don't know how many hours it was on that temperature. Besides, someone messed with my settings and turned it up higher. I was half asleep and panicking that I'd have a baked egg so I turned it way down, quickly. Before the 150 degrees. I don't know what temp it got bumped to—or set at by someone else—or when it happened."

"Well, we do know it was refrigerated at 5.5 degrees Celsius for two hours, then heated at 150 degrees for an unknown amount of time approximately fourteen days, with some unknown variation of temperature."

And just how do you know how long my eggs were refrigerated, Mr. Ben?

#

Once hatched, the chick grew twice as fast as the others. It moulted its pinfeathers the second week, replacing them with magenta body feathers, and flight feathers of red, orange, and bright yellow.

Brittany fed the young bird first, then went out to feed Sparky and the others.

Sparky perked up as she neared, preening his feathers and dropping two on the floor. He suddenly threw his head back, crying out the peacock-like Eh-RAH, Eh-RAH that he was known for. A moment later, every male phoenix in the room threw their heads back and copied the cry. Sparky repeated the cry, then followed it with a series of RAHs that went up and down the scale several times.

He's yodeling, Brittany thought, just before a higher pitched cry answered from the warming room. She dashed back to see her chick standing on a roost, wings outspread and flapping furiously.

My egg hatched a female. My theory was right. She determined not to give any further information until she knew more about the *real* project behind the project. Doug's response to her joke a little over a month ago still bothered her.

#

"Want to go on a supply run? You need to get out more, staring at your female chick all day isn't great for your health." Ben clamped a hand around her wrist and towed her towards the door.

"Sounds good. After my eggs landed in the fridge, I guess I'm just worried about something happening to her."

"Nothing will happen. That's the first female we hatched. She's the most precious bird we have."

"Meet you at the boat in ten, Ben. I have to change my shoes and use the facilities." She headed back up to change her shoes, tucking a glove of pinfeathers in the bottom of her sock before replacing the shoe.

After the boat ride, Brittany offered to help buy supplies.

"Nah, I've got it covered. You know I have a system. I can try to find you some snack food if you want. What are your favorites?"

Brittany listed off some candy and chips, not expecting much result. As she shopped for a brightly colored wrap-dress, the back of her mind kept dreaming up spy-type scenarios. Before she found a dress she liked, she determined not to eat any snacks offered to her, no matter how tempting. She didn't trust anyone on the project, not anymore.

She went into the post office to send the dress back to her parents' home. While there, she found a letter from Amanda in her secret post box.

Brittany –
The turtle box came already opened for a customs search. Isn't that crazy? Thanks for the sculpture. It's so pretty.

I did a little research about archaeopteryx, you're right that they turned up to be part bird, part reptile. I'll pay you the $20 when you get back home. I thought sure the "first bird" was all bird. So much for betting on fossils. Next letter I'll send you a turtle question.

How are things going with Ben? You sounded really excited about him in your last letter. Hope things are doing well, especially if your only other choice is that Doug person. He sounds like bad news, probably has a wife or girlfriend back home somewhere.

We had our big hatching this past month. Turtles, turtles, everywhere. Three different species! Green sea turtles, leatherbacks, and a single nest of really rare Saddleback tortoises. Do you think you could find me sculptures of the other species? I'd really like a complete set that resemble them. If you can't then that's okay, too.

Take care and have fun with your birds.
Love,
Amanda.

Brittany smiled. Amanda could practically read her mind. She headed back to the sculpture booth, pitching the crumpled letter into a grated fire barrel along the way. It caught immediately. She found a land turtle that probably looked nothing like a Saddleback, but the shell opened on a hinge to store things inside. The floor of the compartment lifted if you pulled in the right place. Brittany sat down and removed her shoe, quickly moving the glove into the floor compartment. She replaced it, and closed the hinged lid. A minute or two later, Ben loomed up.

"What are you doing?"

"Taking a rock out of my shoe, what do you think?" She handed him the piece of gravel she'd palmed before sitting down.

"What's this?" He picked up the turtle box. "Another gift for your friend?" He popped open the lid and frowned.

"Should I send her a flower inside it as a surprise? Or put a piece of plastic in to keep the joke going?" She took the box back from him.

"Plastic is better. The flower would never get through customs."

Brittany frowned. "Hm. I didn't think about that." She searched until she found a plastic necklace with birds painted on it. Ben helped her wrap the necklace so it would not rattle, then wrapped her package for her at the post office. She addressed it, and he handed it to the postmaster. Brittany insisted on paying the postage.

"You can't do everything for me, Ben."

"I can certainly try. Let's get back to the boat."

When they reached the boat, Ben double-checked the crates. One was missing. After a long discussion between Ben and some of the locals in some sort of pidgin language, the last crate suddenly found its way to the boat.

Brittany sat quietly on the way back. Ben seemed in a bad mood, a mood that only worsened when they arrived.

Doug waited on the dock with two of the other men, hand and arm wrapped in gauze. His eyes looked glassy, and his speech thick, probably from a strong pain-killer.

"What happened?" Brittany blurted out.

"Bunsen burner accident. Turned out to be the source of our gas leak." The waiting men helped Ben offload as far as the dock, then helped Doug into the boat and ordered Ben to take them to the hospital.

"I can help you carry the crates," Brittany offered.

"We got it," one of the other workers grumbled. "Go feed your stupid birds. Carefully."

She walked nearly halfway up the path when she heard a crash behind her. Glancing over her shoulder, she saw three of the men scrambling to pick up an overturned crate and refill it. *Are those guns?* She looked ahead, concentrating on the main building, and hoped no one had seen her glance back.

Sparky's cage sat empty. Both the lock and the top hinge appeared to be melted, and the door hung loose from one hinge. *Wasn't that why Suzanne left? Sparky burned her and they blamed it on a Bunsen burner incident.*

"Sparky? Sparky." Brittany called out and listened. A muffled noise came from a covered cage in the corner. Brittany peeled back the edge of the cover.

The bars of this cage were twice as thick, the lock more substantial. Sparky stood inside. He appeared to brighten up when he saw her, then hopped around, always returning to the corner closest to the room with the female.

Her heart rose into her throat. Brittany dashed to check on the female.

The female, still unnamed, looked somewhat rumpled. Several feathers lay on the floor of her cage, along with a scorched bit of sleeve. Brittany fed the female first, reaching a finger through the bars to stroke her feathers. The female flinched and backed away, then returned to her meal. An empty carry-cage lay on the floor nearby. *What was Doug doing in here?*

Brittany thought back to all the questions Ben and Doug asked her about calling the birds by name, and how to keep them gentle when she hand-fed them. Doug's panic about her weapons research joke. Ben's crate of guns. It all added up.

They were trying to train the phoenix-birds to go behind enemy lines and set fires. No wonder they were so happy to have the female. They could breed their own eggs, send the eggs to unsuspecting people when they were about to hatch and have the birds wreak havoc inside buildings.

She had to stop this. These beautiful birds, not extinct like everyone thought, but so rare and vibrant with life that they could be mistaken as the "bird of paradise" symbol on

70

the flag. Brittany felt used, used to tame their specimens and write up reports on their behavior, just to make this military operation work better.

She opened Sparky's cage. "Come on, boy." Next she held open the door to the warming room, and approached the female's cage. Sparky flew over and sat on the cage top, hissing at Brittany.

"Hush up. I'm unlocking her cage."

Sparky continued to hiss as Brittany opened the cage door. She took a few steps back.

The female emerged slowly, trying her wings in the open air.

Brittany went back to hold the door open. "Come on, Sparky, bring her out here. Quickly."

Sparky swooped around a few times, then flew through the door. He returned, chirping and yodeling his fluting cry. The female followed tentatively, less used to flying.

Brittany walked across the room and held the outside door open, allowing them to escape into the evening light. She returned inside, carefully closing all the doors and cages, then went up to her room and put the clothes she planned to pack in a loose pile on the end of her bed. The rest she would leave behind, She had little else but her notebooks, and she knew they had been read and re-read for "confidential" information.

Ben got back late at night from dropping Doug and his companions at the hospital. Brittany was ready for him. She ran up to hug him in the outer room, smearing a plant petal across the back of his collar in the process. It left a light, but noticeable perfume.

"I'm not in the mood, Brit." He pushed her away.

"Wait, what's that smell? Is that perfume?" She glowered at him. "I knew it! That's why you didn't want me to help buy supplies. I saw you talking to that girl working by the markets. Is this *her* perfume?" A few people stopped to watch.

"What? No. What are you talking about?"

"Amanda warned me that Doug probably had a girl or a wife, but you? How could you? You acted so interested in me. What were you doing, stringing me along until you got what you wanted?" The crowd grew. With her peripheral vision, Brittany saw Director Hanse walk into the room.

Ben spluttered.

She poked him in the chest with her finger "If I can't trust you, Ben, who can I trust around here? Director Hanse?"

She whirled on her heel, stomping across the room. "I've had it with your overprotectiveness, your patronizing attitude. And now your lies. I'm out of here. I quit!" She stomped off to her room, Director Hanse trailing her.

"You can't just quit, Miss Kay. There are procedures…"

"I don't care about your procedures. I can't work with him anymore. It's *him* or me." She grabbed her duffel bag and stuffed a shirt into it.

"Now wait just a minute. We do sensitive work here, and you have to be searched."

"Fine, search me." She dumped the duffel on the floor. "See, nothing here." She grabbed the clothes from her pile and shook them out, one by one, before stuffing them in the duffel bag. She reached over for another pair of pants, then threw them on the floor. "Hell, I'm done. You can keep the rest of my clothes." She picked up her notebooks and threw them at him. "Check these too. Just yank out the pages I can't take with me."

The last notebook landed open, with a partial letter she wrote to Amanda, extolling all of Ben's wonderful qualities and her expectations that the relationship would soon go to a higher level. The letter finished with the words "It's so nice to have someone I can trust."

The Director read the letter and removed it from the notebook, along with two other pages.

Brittany hoped the Director didn't notice the crease in the notebook's spine that made certain it landed open. She grabbed the notebooks and stuffed them in the top of the duffel, along with a few odds and ends.

"You will remember that you signed a confidentiality agreement."

"Of course I remember that. I can't mention anything about the research—or the Phoenix birds—until a full year after you publish your research and findings. You have all the copies of my behavioral notes already."

"We're down several people right now because of Doug's accident. Can't you stay another week or two?"

"No. I can't work with that lying, cheating… that Ben." She spat the last word out.

"He'll have to take you back to the main island, to the airport."

"You don't have anyone else that can drive the boat? What about a pilot for the helicopter?" She waved her hand in the general direction of the helo pad.

"I can pilot." Hanse looked disappointed.

"Well, good, then we can leave right now."

"It will have to wait for morning. The winds can be treacherous around the islands at night. There's also a cost for fuel."

"Whatever. Keep my paycheck, that should cover it. Daybreak is in what, two hours? I'll sit up and wait."

#

The two hours passed quickly, and after a short discussion where she again turned down an offer to stay, the Director personally flew her back to the airport. She looked down as she left the facility, and silently cried the rest of the way to the airport.

73

"Do not be sad. No man is worth crying over. You are going home." The Director made certain she had her tickets, visas, and passport before he left.

Only after his helicopter left the airport did she smile to herself. The tears were not for Ben, who was apparently involved in something she didn't want to know about, but tears of joy for Sparky and his mate. As they passed a volcano, she had seen two magenta blurs on a pile of rocks, no doubt choosing some for a nest. She did feel sorry for the next researcher, though. Sixteen phoenix males would be maturing within days of each other… and they could be quite competitive. She hoped the rest of the birds would survive.

The Fairy's Invitation

Round the church thrice
Widdershins
Knock three times
I'll let you in
And the place you'll find inside
The Palace grounds where High Lords ride

Dance a night
Under the moon
Trace the air
With mystic runes
Clap my hands before him three times
Come the sun he will be mine

If his true love
Follows him
Whispering prayers
She'll find him
And wearing inside-out her clothes
Her touch will save him and he'll know

Then my spell
Now broken be
He'll follow her
Through sunlit trees
If he marries her before next night
He will never for me fight

[Note: These song lyrics mention many beliefs about fairies.
Circling a church three times anti-clockwise would open a
passage to fairy lands. High Lords refers to the tall slender
Sidhe [Shee] fairies. Wearing clothing inside out kept the
wearer safe from fairy magic, especially glamour (illusion). A
married man would be protected from a female fairy's lure.

75

Grandson of the Moon

Oleia watched her baby carefully. Stubby arms reached up towards the leafy branch over the cradle. The leaves rustled as the breeze—there was a breeze, wasn't there?--wafted past, rippling the grass outside. She relaxed, but only for a moment. She couldn't bear to lose another child...

#

"Now breathe, Oleia, breathe." The midwife took a deep breath, gesturing.

"I can't. Something, huh, huh, something must be wrong. It never hurt this bad before."

"Everything is fine. Now, breathe."

Istan ran into the room, slamming the door. "Just hold off a few hours more, Oleia. The full moon rises tonight!"

The midwife scooted him out of the room. "You're not supposed to be in here. Go, sit, and choose a name."

#

Several hours later, the time came to birth the child.

"Push now, Oleia, push for the life of your child."

With a great heave, Oleia pushed. The child's head squeezed out, resisting all the way. The baby lay lifeless on the bed, the bluish-purple of a ripe plum.

"No no no no no." Oleia grabbed her baby and hugged him close. "Not again." She squeezed his limp body as if she could bring it to life with sheer love.

A line of yellow goop oozed from the child's mouth. The baby twitched when the midwife wiped the goop away.

"Let him go, Oleia, you're squeezing the life out of him." The midwife gently took the child. Goop sprayed from the boy's mouth, followed by a gasp and his first cry. The purplish- blue skin turned angry red, then pink as the midwife laid him across his mother's stomach. "You have a son."

The clouds cleared for a moment, and a thin moonbeam of pure white landed on the boy.

Her husband burst inside. "The moon has marked him." Istan lifted the boy into the air. "You will be strong, a true hero. I name you Judemar."

The moonbeam winked out.

He ran outside, carrying the boy.

Oleia watched through the window. The clouds cleared, yet the moon remained completely dark.

"What happened to the moon?" No sooner did Istan speak the words when the moon reappeared, glowing the faint dark crimson of blood. Istan lifted his gaze to the moon, lowered it to his son, and lifted it again to the moon. After a moment, the moon went dark again.

Istan returned inside and thrust the boy at Oleia. "He's cursed. Look at the moon."

"He's not cursed. The moon's coming back." A slender crescent shone along one edge, slowly widening until the moon regained her full glory an hour later.

#

Judemar's eyes shone a clear light blue for several days, then overnight turned a light brown. Neither color matched Oleia's green eyes or Istan's dark brown.

The same day, he smiled for the first time. She leaned over the cradle, heart melting at his winning smile... until it froze. Judemar smiled not at her, but rather at something unseen in the middle of the room.

A jar of beans inched along a shelf until it fell off the end. A bag of grain followed. The handful of grains that spilled on the floor floated up into the air, spinning round as if caught in a whirlwind. The baby laughed.

Oleia shushed him, scooping him up and walking him around the house until the magic stopped. A wizard for a son; her husband would never accept that.

#

Oleia remained proud of her son, in spite of his odd ways. Judemar walked and spoke early. The boy caught on quickly not to do magic in front of his father.

At three, he threw wet river rocks into the fire to chase away little unseen animals. The rocks exploded into sharp splinters, stabbing her arms and legs. The boy took a wound in the head that knocked him unconscious for two full days.

Much of the magic stopped after that. Judemar no longer smiled and laughed as he had before. He developed a new habit of scrunching up his face and tipping his head sideways. He sat watching the air and the river for hours like that, occasionally smiling.

#

On the boy's fourth birthday, Istan touched his shoulder. "Let me tell you about your namesake, Judemar, the Grandson of the Moon."

Oleia could just hear his words as she boiled wild grapes for jelly.

#

"One day, the Moon came down and landed with a thump. She planned a short visit, but met a handsome farmer.

"Her brothers erupted in fury, and rode stars across the sky to look for her. They did not land so gently. The land cracked, and many houses fell. The sky darkened, and brilliant red sunsets and dawns were the only way the people knew that the Sun had not abandoned them.

"The Moon hid from her brothers, married the handsome farmer, and gave him Selene, a daughter.

"When the girl turned three years old, the skies cleared and the sun shone brightly again. A few months later, the moon returned to the sky.

"Selene grew up and found a husband from a far land. Their only son, Judemar, became a great hero."

#

Their voices faded as the two walked down towards the river. Oleia wished she could have followed them to hear the end of the tale. Instead, she set her two young daughters to squashing small bits of dough. Two and three were perfect ages to learn to knead the bread.

Her husband's angry shouts brought her running from the kitchen.

Istan stood waist-deep in the river, his arm in the water up to his shoulder. Judemar was nowhere to be seen. The ground heaved up, and Istan stumbled backward halfway to shore.

She could see her son in the water now, below the surface. The ground heaved a second time, tossing her husband head over heels onto the grass of the riverbank.

Oleia reached the water's edge and plunged in, grabbing her son by the arm. She pulled and something pulled back. She pulled again. After a third pull, Judemar's head broke the surface. She carried him to the riverbank. He kicked and tried to pull away.

"Mom, I want to play more."

#

A week later, Oleia took her son to see the fortune teller. Her friends warned her that the woman faked card readings, but she'd also heard a time or two about the woman's accuracy. It cost her four jars of jelly to bring the boy inside.

They stepped into the wagon through a curtain of dark red velvet like the nobles wore. A cloth covered a table in the middle of the room, with a small pile of painted pictures to one side and a pointed cut crystal on the other.

"Welcome. What would you know today?" The fortune teller's wrist rattled with beaded bracelets as she reached for the pictures. "Tell me what your problem is."

Oleia plopped her son into the chair. "I need to know his future and what to do."

"I see." The fortune teller spread the pile of pictures out on the table. "You may choose three pictures. Keep them face down."

Oleia watched as her son carefully chose.

"Very good. Now, let me consult my crystal." The woman looked deep within. She began to shake. Her eyes rolled up, showing white.

"I see... I see..." The blood drained from her face. Her voice took on a remote calmness. "Buildings explode in fire. Mud fountains up and buries a house. Black poison coats walls, melting through cloth and skin. Half-melted silver bracelets in rubble. Water grabbing a child and throwing him into thorns."

The fortune teller closed and opened her eyes, then scrambled out of her chair so fast she fell over backward. "Get him away. Take him to a wizard on the other side of the mountains. The son you carry will be normal, but the third daughter will be like this one. Take her to a healer early and let her learn those ways. Now get out!" The fortune teller fled.

"Come, son." Oleia did not want to use the boy's name in this place. "Let the pictures alone."

She stopped and stared. Judemar flipped over his three pictures, smiling. One depicted a burning tower, the second a fountain in a garden, and the third a broken bracelet. How did the fortune teller know which cards he chose? It had to be a trick. The whole session was fake.

They shopped before they went home, trading more jelly for the supplies they needed. She indulged him a little, letting him stand behind the man reading the latest notice aloud. The boy loved to pretend he could read. Not that she or Istan would know if he'd done it properly or not.

Oleia let her son chatter on the way home. Her thoughts kept returning to the fortune teller's recommendation. Bring the boy to a wizard. She would tell her husband, but not yet.

Her son turned five and the crops failed. She bore another healthy son, but needed food herself to nurse him properly. She finally broke down and told her husband about the visit to the fortune teller.

"Bring him to a wizard? That's just what we'll do. We'll sell him for enough to feed the younger ones, and get a start on a new farm."

#

Oleia's mouth sagged at the one-story house with its thatched roof. Surely a wizard could afford a bigger house. Their old farmhouse was bigger than this. She stood at the roadside with the children, two boys, two girls, and another on the way, while her husband waited on the doorstep and then went inside to speak with the wizard.

After far too long a wait, Istan beckoned her to bring the children.

When they reached the door, Oleia knew one thing for certain. This wizard badly needed a housekeeper. Otherwise he seemed nice enough for an old man.

"So these are the children. A fine group. Any others besides the eldest show any sign of powers?"

"None, sir. We've been lucky with the rest." Istan shuffled his feet.

"Luck. Hmm." The wizard turned to Judemar. "Show me what you can do, boy." The boy looked between his father and the wizard, then at the ground.

"Not a very auspicious start."

"Tell him," she urged.

"My dad thinks I'm magic because my toys flew." Judemar frowned. "But I didn't do it. The air animals did, only he can't see them. Or the water animals that played with me when he tried to push me under in the river. Or the ground ones and water ones together that threw him out of the water. It wasn't me."

"Shut up, boy." Istan smacked his son across the cheek, leaving a mark.

"None of that. I'll take the boy, and I'll double the price." The wizard and Istan haggled for a moment more, then the wizard produced two small sacks.

Istan looked delighted. Oleia felt sick.

"Come along, boy." Judemar went inside with the wizard. The door closed and the bolt clicked.

Istan practically danced his way back to the road.

Oleia hung back, listening through the door.

"Are you all right, boy?" The wizard's voice sounded gentle.

"Yes, Mister Wizard, Sir. I'm okay."

"I have plenty of food. I can see you're a growing boy."

"Thank you, Mister Wizard, Sir."

"Call me Haz. And you are?"

"Judemar, named after my father's famous ancestor."

"Jude who? Nevermind, I'll call you Simon."

"Thank you, Haz, Sir."

"Just Haz. Let's make some lunch, Simon."

Oleia stepped away from the door and rejoined her family—what was left of it—by the road. "He'll be okay, I think," she told her husband. She didn't believe her own words. Guilt mounted with every bite of food purchased with the tainted coins.

#

She saw signs even before the child was bom. Phantom hands pushed against her abdomen, to be met with a kick from inside. Jars fell from shelves.

Oleia watched her third little girl carefully. Stubby arms reached up towards the leafy branch over the cradle. The leaves rustled as the breeze—there was a breeze, wasn't there?—wafted past, rippling the grass. She relaxed, but only for a moment. The baby smiled, stare focused in the

82

mid-air. Oleia tensed. Her husband would not take this child away from her. She would not let him. She couldn't bear to lose another one.

Colleen H. Robbins

The Trek to the Hidden Mountain

A far trek north from the Tear Sea's Shore
Through misty swamps slogging with muscles sore
And dodging leeches—the eternal bore
On the Trek to the Hidden Mountain.

The mists seem thicker as daylight grows
Twining about us--our trek it slows
And we can't see anything under our nose
On the Trek to the Hidden Mountain.

A wailing cry, a mad thing's yell
Like a soul tormented in deepest hell
If we don't meet the crier 'tis just as well
On the Trek to the Hidden Mountain.

A man appears—their leader I deem
Standing astraddle his small bireme
From his mouth we hear that fearful scream
On the Trek to the Hidden Mountain.

"We're Mountain men" the madman cries
Swatting a bit at the bloodthirsty flies
"And on our ship your clothes can dry."
Oh—the Trek to the Hidden Mountain.

The men appear... Then gone again
We drifted through that dismal fen

Just beginning to wonder when...
And we saw the Hidden Mountain.

Their warriors journey far, it seems
Home and gone like drifting dreams
A'viking up and down the streams
Such is life in the Hidden Mountain.

The mountain we saw—then we were gone
We knew for sure 'twould not be long
'fore we dreamed of the echoing mountain song
The Song of the Hidden Mountain.

Shalla

Arlo braced himself with his staff, then fumbled the small leather roll out of his pocket. The faded picture remained the same: a three-pointed star, each point a detailed mountain, with their bases surrounding a triangular valley. Shalla Valley, if the tales—and the map—were correct. He turned the map twice, then rolled it up and put it away. Two year's journey through this land, and he clung less than fifty feet from his goal.

A week before, he spotted a mountain that closely resembled one from his map. This section of the range had clusters of six and seven mountains that practically grew out of each other, the passes between them high enough to be dusted with snow in this early summer season. The closest mountain, sheer and stark against the sky, bore no resemblance to the map, so he circled its base, and circled again to reach the pass connecting the proper mountain to the one beyond.

Concentrating now, he grasped a protruding rock with his left hand, then released his staff to swing beneath him on its rope and searched for another handhold with his right. Found a foothold, then another. Stood, and moved his hands again, over and over until he crested the connecting ridge. He grasped his staff again and moved across patches of snow to what should be the valley of Shalla.

Trees and rocks on the slope beneath him, and a spectacular river carving its way down the opposite side. No village, no smoke, and no sign of any trails. The valley between—more of a canyon, really—traced its long, thin way past the base of the mountain.

Arlo went through the motions of making camp, his thoughts overflowing with disappointment. *Have I thrown away my life on a false quest? The soothsayers seemed so sure.*

###

Arlo and the other village children watched a large bird with long legs spear frogs in the nearby pond. A floating log transformed into a monster with large teeth and attacked the bird. The bird pulled away and fluttered onto the shore. The log-monster crawled out of the pond like a giant lizard, sending all the children fleeing for their parents. All, that is, except Arlo.

He crept toward the bird, making soothing noises. Its leg bent strangely, and blood spotted one wing. When the log monster came closer, he threw rocks at it until it returned to the pond. Keeping an eye out for the monster, he gathered the bird up in his arms and brought it to the healer-woman just outside the village.

"The monster hurt it. Can you fix it?" Arlo held the bird out to her.

The bird stabbed out at the healer with its beak, drawing blood from her arm.

"Now, now, Master Crane, you know I'm only going to help you."

With Arlo's help, she straightened and bound the crane's leg, and stitched the wound on its wing. By the time they finished, a group of villagers brought in two men injured while removing the monster from the pond.

The healer turned to Arlo. "You have a gentleness about you, and a deeper understanding than most. You should go to Shalla and become a priest."

Arlo's father pushed forward. "A priest? My son? Never. He'll be a warrior and a farmer, like the rest of us."

#

The mountain's chill ate into Arlo's bones in spite of his banked fire, so he sat up and watched the night sky. The stars shone bright enough to see across his small camp with no difficulty. Trying to pick out the few patterns he knew, he watched in wonder as a star flew across the sky, followed shortly by another, and another. *Something important is going to happen to me*. For hours the stars flew, and Arlo fell into a deep sleep.

He woke up with frost on his blanket and renewed optimism. After eating a scant breakfast from the food he carried, he melted some snow to refill his water and turned for one last look around. The beauty surrounding him infused him with energy. The raging river, the back side of the mountain he thought was on his map, and—his mouth sagged open.

The mountain beyond—a mountain he had walked past—closely matched *another* mountain on his map. But that would put it next to the first mountain face. Confused, he pulled out the map again. He cupped the leather in his hands, the triangular valley in the bottom. The three mountainsides faced *inside* the valley, not toward the outside world. He grabbed his staff and headed back.

#

The trails near the valley, rough with rocks and tree roots, reminded him of the roads between villages back home. His father took him trading to three other villages when he turned sixteen. They passed two other places along the way, long abandoned and tumbled into ruins. Arlo wondered what happened to the people. When they reached the living villages, he watched with wide eyes and tried to see everything at once in the busy marketplaces. He noticed people dipping feathers in ink and making marks on some kind of thin tree bark. By the third village, he could not rein in his curiosity.

"What are those marks for?" He gestured at the bark piece in front of a young man scarcely older than himself.

"They are letters. This woman wishes to tell her sister about her new baby. The message will be sent to the city

88

and her sister will read it, or have someone read it to her, so that she can hear the news."

Arlo leaned over, bringing his ear close to the letter. "I do not hear anything. How do they hear the news?"

"You must learn to read them, so they will speak inside your head. There are many lands and many types of letters and runes."

"Ruins? I have seen some of those."

"You should go to the Shalla Valley and learn. You see more than most."

"I have been told that before. How do I get there?"

"They are in the mountains far to the east. I shall draw you a map. Have you any paper?"

Arlo pointed at the pile of thin bark. "Is that paper?" At the letter-maker's nod, Arlo shook his head. "I have only this." Arlo pulled out a scrap of thin leather he carried to repair rips in his trousers.

"That will do nicely." The letter-maker began to draw, but Arlo's father came back for him. Arlo winced as the man's hand clamped painfully on his shoulder.

"I need you to carry things. Come along."

The letter-maker tossed Arlo the leather scrap. "Remember, to the east, where the sun rises."

#

After a long and difficult climb, Arlo stopped on the inside of the pass. A large temple complex stretched out in the triangular valley below. Numerous people moved between the buildings. Farther out, gardens and small farms dotted two of the valley's corners, and a small lake filled the third.

A robed man limped up to meet him and bowed. "You are welcome in your quest for knowledge. I am Hannan."

"Thank you, Hannan. I am Arlo. Where do I start learning?"

Hannan broke into a grin. "You have come to the right place. Follow me."

They descended the long path into the valley, where the square temples turned out to be workrooms and gathering places, and the long, thin halls between temples were lined with small rooms on each side.

Hannan steered Arlo to the hallway. "Choose where you wish to sleep and sometimes study. We have few students right now. When there are many, we share our rooms until the floor can hold no more."

Arlo chose a room and left his meager belongings. Hannan explained the mealtime routines as they returned outside. Following a trail, they passed a maze of partial walls, all that was left of a ruined building.

"Will I study there as well?"

"That decision is for the Master. Come, with me." Hannan led Arlo to a trail that snaked up the side of the mountain. "The Master awaits."

Arlo could barely make out a man standing on a ledge high above. "Up there?" he pointed, then turned to Hannan. The robed man limped back toward the temple complex, well along that path.

Tired and hungry, Arlo began his climb. The trail seemed easy enough, with only a few steep areas. After half an hour, he reached the ledge.

The Master stood looking over the valley. "Come, stand with me. What do you see?"

Arlo shuffled forward. The sun dipped toward the mountains. The temple buildings, arranged as eyes and a mouth with the hallways dropping down from the outside edges, were bisected by the growing shadows. The ruins looked like a jumble of sticks. Beyond, the forests and waterfalls on the mountain disappeared in the growing shadows.

"The mountains are very beautiful."

"And?"

"The temples are oddly arranged, but pleasing to the eye."

"Do you see nothing else?"

"No. What should I be looking for?"

The Master bowed his head. "What are you here to study? What do you wish to learn?"

"I want to learn about letters and ruins."

"Sinta shall teach you. Come back and speak to me in a month's time of your progress."

#

Arlo climbed to the ledge, eager to share his new-found knowledge. His student's robe gave him a little trouble on the steep areas, but he tucked the long robe up into his belt.

"Welcome again, Arlo."

"Hello, Master. I have learned most of my letters, and can make out some words now. It is often difficult."

"Yet you persist. Has Sinta shown you any runes yet?"

"Not the ruins in the valley, but word-pictures that he calls runes. Each one means an entire word of sounds."

"Stand with me and watch the sunset. What do you see?"

"The same things that I saw before."

The Master bowed his head, a slight frown upon his face. "Come find me again after five months."

#

"You have been here for six months now, Arlo. How do you fare?"

"I can read all of my letters, and puzzle out many words, but I do not know what all of them mean. I went to the ruins on my own, and found many word-pictures drawn there. Some of them had other meanings, like gates and doorways.

"Doorways?" The Master's eyes glinted. "And what doorways have you found?"

His hands clasped, Arlo thought hard. "I have seen doorways in the temple, doorways that lead to knowledge. Letters and runes are doorways themselves, doorways to the voices of the past. Even the rising and setting of the sun are doorways to each day, spelling out the weather if you know how to read them."

"Very good. Now tell me what you see."

Arlo looked across the valley. A brilliant red sunset tinted the cliffs in shades of red and purple. The fertile fields below glowed lush and green. Even the buildings had their place. Against the greenery, their brown and grey stones stood out like letters on a page.

Letters. The building shapes spelled out a simple word: THINK.

Think? Think about what? Think much, think little. Concentrate. Consider. So many meanings to the word. Not as simple as he first thought.

"Arlo?"

"Apologies, Master. I was thinking."

"And what do you see?"

He was about to answer when he glanced at the ruined building. Sticks and branches lay randomly about near half-burned timbers. The wind gusted and nudged a branch back into place. Arlo blinked. The randomness vanished and the rune for doorway stood out as he had never seen it before. Artfully arranged. Purposely so.

"I see that thinking can lead to a doorway, even in the midst of nature's randomness, just as over-thinking can obscure one."

The Master smiled. "You are a true brother of Shalla. Be welcome."

They stood together, watching the sunset fade, grateful for the coming rains to aid the gardens. A fresh, new beginning. The perfect weather to begin his exploration of the newly discovered doorway in the morning.

The Scribe's Forgotten Pen

The Scribe's forgotten pen
Lies gathering dust near dried-out inkwells
The scroll half-finished
Fades to illegibility, forever unread

Where are the hands
To scribe the words the mind dictates?
Where are the minds
To dream of tales for other minds to read?

A single lonely hand
Lifts the pen from the table and scrawls
The beginnings of a new scroll
Hoping to be joined by others.

Pastoral Plus

Ranch and Farm co-exist
For the first time in history

The last humans are gone

Their Hatfield / McCoy style feud
Forever at peace

Horses
Run free
Saddles gone
Leaping fences
Still protected
By the heirs
Forever

Centaurs wear ten-gallon hats
Shirtless as they drive cattle

Minotaurs plow the fields

Satyrs play their reed pipes
Guiding sheep and goats home

Unicorns Rear Up

Unicorns rear up,
Their virgin captors riding
Forgotten freedom.

Chasing Rainbows

Reyna Manoa drove along the highway, dodging around cars and weaving between trucks as she tried to catch up to the rainbow. I-290 through Chicago was so backed up she should have stopped. Her therapist said she should have stopped months ago when Richard left her, or maybe when Iris first disappeared.

A truck slowed, blocking her view of the rainbow. *I might as well get off the highway*, she thought. *I'll never find her now.*

She exited and pulled into an Exxon station near the end of the off-ramp. The attached mini-mart was doing brisk business. Thirsty after the long drive, a Coke sounded good to her.

She stepped down into one of the puddles that covered the parking lot. Coins crunched under her shoes. "See a penny, pick it up," she murmured. *I need all the luck I can get.* The sun broke through the clouds as she picked up the first coin. The puddle fluoresced with an oily rainbow that broke up as she lifted the coin.

"Watch your step, ma'am." A man in a red pickup truck wiped oil from the soles of his shoes with a handful of paper napkins. "Some yahoo let his car leak all over the place. There's oil on the sidewalk, too."

"Thanks for the warning." Reyna picked her way across the parking lot and hesitated at the curb. Oily footprints covered the sidewalk. Smaller tracks, maybe from sparrows, crossed the concrete and led to the shelter of the nearby bushes.

She mounted the curb and reached for the door. A skittering noise made her turn. For a second, she thought she saw a frog disappearing under the bush. A frog with dead white hands.

Oh, God, I'm hallucinating again. Just like the day Iris disappeared: a flash of color as her daughter ran through the base of the rainbow, a flash of dead white hands grasping the child's shoulders when she vanished.

"You going in or not?"

Reyna jumped at the unexpected voice and sidled onto the grass. "Be my guest." She let the gaggle of teenagers pass, all madly texting away, and fled to her car.

She fiddled with the radio before heading up the on-ramp. *The newscaster's voice is pleasant, even though the news isn't.* More war news, another kidnapping, and a mysterious disease sweeping through the Tribal reservations. When the weather report came on, she paid more attention.

"A few days of gorgeous sunshine ahead, folks, followed by a thunderstorm late Thursday or early Friday morning. For you sky watchers, we've got solar flares predicted for the next few days, increasing in intensity and bringing down a brilliant display of the Aurora Borealis that should be visible as far south as Saint Louis by the end of the week."

Reyna stopped listening. She had to get home to watch the Weather Channel, see where the storm was supposed to hit. One of the storms would have the right rainbow, the rainbow that would return Iris.

The next turnoff was a mile away when her seatbelt snapped open. The thin wavering tone from the dashboard distracted her almost as much as fumbling with the recalcitrant clip. She exhaled and slid the clip in just as the belt tightened. A horn blared. Reyna swerved back into her lane.

The back passenger window hummed as it rolled down in its frame. Reyna stabbed at the button on her armrest and brought it back up again. Her fingers danced on the rest as the windows randomly rolled up and down. She glanced into the next lane and caught sight of something small and green on the passenger armrest. It dropped down the far side of the seat before she could get a better look.

She took the next exit. Something scampered over her foot, prickly little claws snagging in her rainbow-colored socks. She shrieked and pressed the brakes. The pedal resisted for a second before collapsing to the floor with a pop. Instantly her foot was soaked with warm, sticky fluid as the car skidded to a halt.

Reyna struggled with the door, pressing the unlock button several times before she got the handle open. She jumped outside and whirled around as her purse tipped and crashed to the floor. Lipstick, hairbrush, and change purse spilled out; the latter opening in a rattle of coins. She rounded the car and jerked the passenger door open. She bent down and savagely gathered her change when she noticed the flashing lights behind her.

"Do you need any help, ma'am?"

Reyna stood slowly. The officer stood a few inches taller than she did, with a face that came straight out of her dreams. He looked just like Richard, but with dark hair. His ring finger was bare. She realized her mouth hung open and closed it.

"Ma'am? Is your foot all right?"

Reyna looked down. Neon green fluid splattered her shoe and sock. "I dropped my slushy." *Stupid excuse.*

She watched mutely as half a dozen froglike creatures scampered away from her car while the officer wrote her a ticket.

#

Reyna sat curled in her favorite rainbow-colored armchair— the same chair she curled in for comfort after Iris disappeared—and watched the flames flicker in the hearth. *They were some sort of supernatural creatures*, she decided. Distracted from the rainbows for the first time in a year, Reyna struggled to make sense of what had happened.

"What do I know about them?" Her words echoed over the sound of the dishwasher. She had spoken aloud. *There's no one to hear me; why not speak aloud?* "They have white arms like the thing that took my Iris." She ticked her fingers as she spoke. "They came from the rainbows in the puddles. They harassed me in my car. They fled after my change purse spilled."

Reyna got up and added another log to the fire, then retrieved her purse from the bookshelf and snuggled back in her chair. "What was it about my change that frightened them?" Pushing aside a wooden tray filled with ceramic rainbows, she dumped an array of silvery coins on the end table. Two dimes and a few nickels hid between the quarters.

Silver, of course. It worked against werewolves in the tales. Why not against other creatures?

She popped out of her chair and headed for the door, then returned long enough to set the firescreen across the hearth and put on her shoes.

Five minutes later she pulled up at the bank. She practically danced her way inside. She still grinned so hard her face hurt when she handed the withdrawal slip to the teller.

"I'd like it entirely in silver quarters, please."

The teller was young, perhaps still in high school. "Quarters aren't silver anymore, Ms. Manoa."

"Fine, give me regular quarters." Reyna drummed her fingers on the countertop, her grin fading.

The teller glanced down at the slip, then back up at Reyna. "Ms. Manoa, we don't keep this many quarters on site. Let me call my manager over, alright? She can help you make a special order."

It took the better part of the afternoon to convince the bank manager that she needed four thousand dollars' worth of quarters. Once the order was in, Reyna spent the balance of Monday afternoon shopping for nets. She finally chose a bow-net sized for catching and banding sparrows and bought five of them: The mesh looked fine enough to capture little white-armed frogs.

#

She picked her quarters up on Wednesday, amazed at the weight of four hundred rolls of coins. She staggered to the car several times, drawing remarks from onlookers. Two rough-looking teens were approaching when she finally jumped in her car and locked the doors. Her shocks squealed all the way home. She left the quarters in the trunk along with the collapsed bow-nets and an old toolbox.

Reyna flipped on the weather report while she opened the last can of tuna for lunch.

"It's clear and warm today, with highs forecast in the 80s and lows in the 60s tonight. A high-pressure system will help that clear weather last until Friday morning, giving us a great chance to catch the Aurora Borealis after a short storm on Friday afternoon. Back to you, Carl."

Reyna flipped off the radio. No rain meant no rainbows. How could she capture the creatures and force them to give Iris back without a rainbow? She paced around the kitchen, dropping bits of tuna sandwich in her wake.

The telephone rang. Reyna jumped, the last bit of sandwich arcing high across the kitchen to land on top of the upper cabinets. She grabbed the phone.

"Hello?" The caller ID was blank. *Got to remember to get that fixed.*

"Reyna? It's Richard."

"What do *you* want?"

"The bank called me a little while ago. Is everything all right over there?

"Everything's just fine except the weather." She paused and listened to Richard breathing.

"I'm coming over, Reyna. This has got to stop."

"Don't bother. I'm going out." Reyna slammed down the receiver. *Oh, god, he's coming over.* She grabbed her keys and purse.

She drove in circles for an hour before she pulled up at the park. It was empty of children at this time of day, the younger ones napping while their mothers watched soap operas, and the older ones still in school. The sun washed the benches with sparkling light. Everything looked fresh and clean, from the empty playground to the cracked marble fish fountain that was not yet turned on for the season.

She drove a second loop around the park, afraid that Richard might track her down. When she reached the fountain again, she slowed.

Iris loved to dance by the fountain in her rainbow-striped sundress. "I'm chasing rainbows;" she said, and ran giggling through the mist. Who ever expected a rainbow to take her?

Reyna drove over the curb and parked on the grass. Could she do it? She rummaged through the toolbox and found a rusty plumber's wrench. She tucked the wrench through her belt and struggled with the bow-nets. Laying them out in a circle around the old fountain, she tried to assemble them. Two trips to the car later, one for a screwdriver and the other for a second copy of the directions after the first one blew away, she finally finished setting them up. With a gentle tug, Reyna could pop the nets up and over, hopefully tangling the little frog-sized creatures.

Next she lugged out the quarters and laid them in the fountain's basin. Reyna sat on the edge of the dry fountain, picking at the plastic wrappings of each roll. Her fingernail popped off. *Damn, another five dollars gone. Acrylics are so expensive.* The wrapping split and quarters flew everywhere. She grabbed the next roll.

By the time she unwrapped ten rolls, her fingers hurt. She went back to the car for a hacksaw blade and tore open the rest. She arranged the coins carefully, filling the basin but allowing the water spouts to stay clear. She pulled the wrench from her belt; marched over to the pipeline, and hooked the wrench over the pipe.

The wrench slipped easily along the metal. She tried to secure it, but the wrench was too large. Frustrated again, she banged the pipe twice. A drop of water oozed out of the joint.

The water was already on. Reyna felt her cheeks warm. She went back over the pipes, following them to the fountain. She crawled under a bush where the pipe went through and almost bumped her nose on a simple shut-off lever. She grabbed hold and twisted. The fountain came on in a sparkle of sunlit rainbows.

The first creatures hopped out within minutes. They resembled yellow hobgoblins this time, eight inches tall with long warty noses. They tore easily through her nets. The hobgoblins danced around the fountain as joyfully as Iris had, picking up coins and vanishing. The rainbow grew brighter.

For every quarter that vanished into the rainbow, another three hobgoblins came out. The quarters were helping them! She raced for the fountain shut-off.

The hobgoblins swarmed over the edge of the fountain and sank claws into her ankles. Reyna fell within an arm's reach of the bushes. She grabbed hold of a branch and pulled. The branch broke loose in her grip as the hobgoblins yanked her backward. She dug her elbows into the mulch beneath the bushes. The scent of cedar mixed with manure invaded her lungs and choked her. She kicked her feet, reached out, and dragged herself forward two inches. She lost an inch as the hobgoblins clawed at her feet. Another inch, two, three she crawled. Her hand closed on the shut-off valve. She twisted as hard as she could.

The patter of water stopped, but the hobgoblins did not. They dragged Reyna back towards the fountain, pummeling her. with tiny fists and scratching her with kitten-claw fingernails. When she bumped up against the cracked marble, she got her knees under her. She heaved to her feet, scattering hobgoblins in every direction.

The rainbow grew stronger than ever, its existence now independent of the water. More hobgoblins popped from the shimmering colors: Reyna dug her hands into the basin and scattered coins on the grass behind her.

The hobgoblins gave a shrill scream, a hiss of escaping air very like the day she overcooked hotdogs in the microwave. She shoveled another handful of coins away from the basin. The rainbow dimmed.

"Hey! Free money!" A child of ten or so, leading the pack of children returning from school, darted up and retrieved a handful of coins from the grass. His friends descended on Reyna. They scooped coins from the basin into backpacks and lunch pails, stuffed their pockets full of quarters and even slid some into their socks and shoes.

Sometime during the chaos the hobgoblins vanished, as did the rainbow. Reyna scraped the last few quarters into a discarded sandwich bag and went home.

Richard waited in the driveway. "Reyna, what happened? Where is all the money you took from the bank?"

She sighed. Of course he asked about the money. "I gave it all away."

"You're not thinking about suicide, are you? That would sully Iris' memory." He laid a hand on her shoulder.

"Don't talk to me about Iris. You never believed me, never helped me try to find her." She slapped his hand away. "Get away from me. Iris isn't dead. The creatures took her—those horrible rainbow creatures." Her ankles throbbed.

Richard caught Reyna as she collapsed. "Let's get you cleaned up and you can tell me about it."

#

Reyna woke to the distant growl of thunder. Her stomach clenched as the thunder growled again. *No*, she realized, *my stomach is growling*.

She sat up, disoriented. Late morning sunshine peeked from between the rainbow-colored curtains. She could hear Richard's soft voice from the hallway.

"Okay, I'll bring her in on Monday. Thanks."

She rounded the corner. Richard tapped his phone. He saw her and took a short, quick step away.

"How are you feeling?"

"Hungry. I can't believe I slept for so long. I have to check the weather, see where the storm will be tomorrow."

Richard touched her gently on the shoulder. "Reyna, it's Friday. You slept for almost two days. Sit down and I'll get you something to eat."

"Friday? How can it be Friday already? I have to close the gates before more children vanish."

While Richard clattered in the kitchen, she grabbed a book from the shelf. Katherine Brigg's "An Encyclopedia of Fairies." She flipped through: hobgoblins, leprechauns, no rainbows. She snapped the book shut. A second book, this one on Norse mythology, spoke of the rainbow bridge Bifrost, but she didn't have any frost giants handy. A pamphlet titled "Rainbows of the Hawaiian Manoa Valley" was more useful. The legend of the Rainbow Princess gave her some ideas. She might not be a princess, but she carried a Hawaiian name. It would have to do.

Reyna scribbled on a scrap of paper. She based her words on the legendary princess' original plea, but instead of attracting the rainbow gates, she planned to close them. Now for the feast.

She barely tasted the sandwich that Richard handed to her in the kitchen. Wilted lettuce and microwave meals in the fridge, a half-eaten jar of peanut butter on the counter next to the empty bread bag, and a handful of canned food: nothing Hawaiian.

"I have to go shopping."

"I noticed. Do you want company?"
Reyna thought about the squeaky shocks in her car. No, she didn't want to deal with Richard's reaction. "Fine. We'll take your car."

At the grocery store, Reyna tossed a can of sliced pineapple and another containing a small ham into a basket, along with a woven placemat and some Macadamia nuts.

"Aren't you going to get some actual food?" Richard asked.

"Later. This is more important."

Her next stop was a Florist. Richard dropped her at the door and drove off to find parking.

Reyna ran up to the clerk. "I need a lei." The young man behind the counter blinked at her and smiled. "The Hawaiian necklace kind."

"Oh, sorry. Those are special orders, take about ten days." He handed her a long form. "Just fill this out for me."

Reyna left the form on the counter and ran from the shop. The clouds were getting thicker.

Richard was just locking the car. "Where to next?"

"K-Mart, I guess."

She checked the toy department first. A dozen pink plastic leis hung on a peg next to the western sheriff play sets.

She held the leis up in front of Richard. "Which do you think are the best two?"

"Reyna, stop this. Iris is gone."

"I'm not doing this for Iris, I'm doing it for me!" Tears stung her eyes. He *still* didn't believe her. She chose two leis at random and dashed to the perfume counter. Richard trailed in her wake.

"I need something Hawaiian;" she told the salesclerk. Reyna waved the leis in the air. "Whatever these are supposed to smell like."

"Chanel Number Five is made from the Ylang-Ylang flower of Hawaii. Would you like the one-ounce bottle?"

Reyna reached into her purse. "That will do perfectly."

Richard refused to look at her when they got back into the car. "I can't believe you just spent two hundred and fifty dollars on a little bottle of perfume."

Reyna stared out the window. Storm clouds built rapidly, their undersides already flickering with lightning.

"Just drop me off at home. You don't need to stay."

"Whatever you want."

Reyna ran up the driveway to the house. The first raindrops splattered on her forehead. She didn't have much time.

She dumped the knickknacks off of the wooden tray, wincing as two of the ceramics clacked together. Reyna tucked the woven fabric of the mat into the tray and arranged ham, pineapple slices, and macadamia nuts in little piles. Thunder boomed closer and closer. She poured the perfume on the leis, thoroughly soaking them, and felt her gorge rise at the overpowering scent of flowers. Gagging, she opened the window and sucked in the rain-freshened air. A wrap-skirt from the back of her closet, a parrot and rainbow print in brilliant colors that she last wore the day Iris disappeared completed her preparations.

The storm passed by, lightning still flickering in the distance like an old fluorescent tube.

When the sun broke through-the clouds, Reyna was ready.

The rainbow arced down from the sky. She hopped into her car and chased after it. Too soon she seemed to be catching up. Rainbows could be tricky that way. Only when she realized the rainbow started down in the park did she swerve and run her car up onto the curb.

The rainbow's end slid down from the sky and touched ground near the old marble fountain. The colors wavered a moment and then grew stronger. *There must still be coins in the grass.* She jumped out of her car, grabbed the tray, and marched toward the end of the rainbow.

Large white hands groped out from the colors and then receded. Reyna laid the tray directly before the rainbow, put on one lei, and tossed the other into the heart of the rainbow. It hung in mid-air.

Kneeling, she lifted her arms. "Hear my plea, oh gods of my daughter's ancestors. I, Reyna Manoa, share my feast with you. I ask a boon from you. Close the portals to my land." The white hands froze in place. The rainbow shivered like sheer curtains in the breeze.

Reyna took a deep breath. "Hear my plea, oh gods of my daughter's ancestors. I, Reyna Manoa, share my feast with you. I ask a boon from you. Close the portals to my land." The colors grew brighter. Reyna could just make out a misty figure in the rainbow. It grew as she watched until it towered over her. She lowered her gaze to the empty tray.

"Hear my plea, oh gods of my daughter's ancestors. I, Reyna Manoa, share my feast with you." The tiny voice echoed her words. A second figure moved forward beneath the legs of the first. Heartbeat pounding, Reyna recognized the girl. "I ask a boon of you." *Oh, god, was Iris still alive in there?* More figures moved behind the girl. Reyna stared at the closest, a white-skinned humanoid with an elephant's trunk protruding from its forehead. Weapons bristled from its belt.

Reyna took another breath, trying to calm herself. Another few words and the portals would be closed. Iris stepped back. Elephant men streamed past her, one by one. Three, four, five stepped out. Reyna couldn't wait any longer.

"Mommy?"

It *was* Iris. She reached out a trembling hand to her daughter.

A heavy weight hit Reyna's back and sent her sprawling face first in the muddy grass. The wooden tray flipped over, catching her across the forehead. Her lei broke and landed in the mud.

"Reyna, get up." Richard climbed off of her.

Reyna stared up at the rainbow receding into the sky. The portals remained open. The elephant creatures...

The elephant creatures surrounded them. Less humanoid than she thought, the creatures each held four weapons. The trunk sported a pair of mandibles set just inside the tip, bristling with jagged teeth.

She scrambled to her feet, hands clutching a mix of coins and muddy grass. She threw them at the nearest-elephant and charged forward. The elephant's arms swung up in an arc that blocked the coins and mud. Reyna ducked and ran beneath, pelting across the wet grass to the car.

She jerked open the door. Something grabbed her skirt.

She shrieked and fumbled with the tie, leaving her skirt behind as she hopped into the car and accelerated. She glanced up at the rearview mirror to see Richard standing with her muddy skirt dangling from his fingers. Reyna whipped the car around, leaving skid marks in the grass. She pushed the door open. "Get in!"

Richard dove into the car as an elephant swung a heavy wooden club at him. The passenger window shattered.

Reyna sped off, door bouncing on its hinges. She drove off the curb, turning so the door swung shut, and raced down the street. The five elephants fell behind.

Richard said nothing until they were safely inside the house: He started a fire and collapsed in Reyna's chair.

"What in the world were those?" His white-knuckled hands gripped the armrests.

"Oh, just rainbow creatures." Her shaking hands belied her casual tone. "I told you about them."

"I guess you did." His voice dropped to a whisper. "Did I see Iris in the rainbow?"

"I don't know. I wanted it to be her but rainbows are tricky." She ran her hands over his shoulders. "You're tense."

"Damn straight." He pulled her down for a kiss.

The door burst open with a crash. The first of the elephants charged in, swords and club swinging. Richard grabbed a piece of kindling and tried to block the blades. "Get out of here, Reyna! I'll hold them."

Reyna ran into the kitchen and yanked open the knife drawer. Empty. The dishwasher was still full. She pulled at the latch, but it refused to slide. She opened the fridge instead and started throwing things, the rain of frozen dinners and ice cube trays driving the elephants back a few steps. *Oh, yes, they're coming for me.*

Richard swung from behind with his kindling. The elephant whirled and clubbed him to the floor. Blood pooled beneath his limp form.

Furious, Reyna threw the last of the ice cube trays and opened the cabinets. A can of peas hit the closest elephant between the eyes and the creature sagged to the floor. "That's for Richard."

A can of spinach hit another in its upper right shoulder. It squealed in agony and backed away. "That's for pushing past Iris."

Reyna's hand closed on empty air. Damn, she still needed to go shopping. She ran out the back door and started across the yard. *Richard. I can't leave him to the creatures.* Circling around the house, she ran in the smashed front door and headed for the fireplace.

The cast iron poker was heavier than she remembered. She lifted it to her shoulder, ankles apart, and took a softball swing. *Crack*. The poker smashed past the elephant's sword and caught it across the face. It sank to the floor in a puddle of white ooze. She heaved the poker back up across her shoulder.

The second elephant feinted twice with the swords and caught her across the ribs with the club. She dropped the iron poker on its foot. The elephant bellowed once and fell backward as its foot dissolved.

In pain, she recovered the poker and threatened another elephant. It backed into a corner. She jumped back as it swung its weapons, then threw the poker at its feet. Again, the touch of the metal had a lethal effect.

She bent to pick up the poker and the side of her head exploded in pain.

The last elephant swung its club back and stepped toward her.

She tried to throw the poker at its feet, but her arm wouldn't work right. Her ribs hurt and she couldn't breathe. She fell to her knees, the poker rolling from her fingers. The elephant jumped backward, away from the deadly metal. Metal clattered as the creature backed into the fireplace tools. It howled once and collapsed. Reyna fell forward.

#

A damp cloth on her forehead woke Reyna. She rolled over and groaned. Richard smiled, a bloody strip of bandage wound around his head.

"We won." He dabbed at her forehead again. "Or rather, *you* did. I wasn't much help."

"They're gone. That's the important thing. At least until they find the next rainbow to come through."

"This is what you've been talking about all this time. These are what took Iris." At her nod, Richard took her hand. "I have an idea. Let's go watch the sky. It's a nice, clear night, no rainbows at all."

He helped her to her feet. They hobbled past pools of white ooze and dark blood, through the broken front door, and out to the front steps.

Reyna groaned as she sat down. The world spun and she grasped the handrail. *Broken ribs, concussion, I'm a mess.*

"Hey, look at the aurora. I've never seen one before."

Reyna looked up. Glowing green tendrils spread across the sky. Red and blue tendrils joined them. Reyna screamed as the entire night sky became a writhing rainbow.

Colleen H. Robbins

Jousting with Unicorns

"I have never jousted unicorns," said she.

"I've only had mine for a year, a gift on High Feast Day."
"It is high time you learned," said he.

He knew the curly-haired, tow-headed girl
--no proper princess like her long-haired sister--
would rather swing a sword, or climb, or run.

She had only sat her unicorn a few times,
just long enough for a few tentative steps.
He checked her seat when she mounted,
corrected the placement of her hands.

They rode one beside the other, slowly at first,
broke into great leaping strides across the leaves and vines
until they crashed through the edge of the forest
into a meadow lush with grass and flowers.
She marveled at the butterflies.

He turned in the grass, his unicorn the enemy now;
she held her seat through pawing forelegs and clashing
horns
tumbled unceremoniously to the ground,
scraping her knee. Blood dripped to feed the soil.

"I won!" shouted the Prince, for he was her brother
and she his sister: stubborn, fierce, and never to admit
defeat,
remounted without aid.

She drove his unicorn back, step by hard won step,
recovered her power as he fell.

Remounting, recounting the bout as their unicorns brought them home.

Colleen H. Robbins

Our Men Have Gone to War

The kings call—our men to the Crusades go,
Out to deserts where sands do blow,
Armed with sword and shield, or bow—
Our men have gone to war.

We women, left behind at home,
Must bring up our young sons alone,
Unknowing where their fathers roam—
Our men have gone to war.

We struggle to keep our homes together,
Hope for the crops that we have rainy weather,
Embroider a pillow, stuff in the last feather--
Our men have gone to war.

Our men will return—that's what they say.
We wait for years, day by day,
Trying to keep the loneliness at bay--
Our men are still at war.

Samurai

Refrain:
>   Fighter strike and Piper blow
>   But Samurai stand clear
>   For though your sword has skill enow
>   To my heart you're dear.

I had a dream, a vision it may
You were surrounded by foes
And only when they lay all dead at your feet
Only then did it close.

R

I saw you standing in a battle fierce
And then I saw you fall
But no sword came to take your life
You'd killed your enemies all.

R

Oh, Samurai, the fight you love
And battle is your art
But to a girl who cautions you back
You could never give your heart.

>   So Fighter strike and Piper blow
>   And Samurai go to war
>   I'll keep you safe with love enow
>   And battle glory shall be yours.

It shall be yours.

Frostbite and Chicken Legs: A Baba Yaga tale

She was dancing with her father's spirit in the frozen meadow by the riverside when the Vikings found her. Whirling and spinning, she chased the spirals of snowflakes caught up by the wind, the spirals that remained behind each of Ymir's invisible footsteps.

The moaning wind carried Ymir's spirit back to the glacier. She collapsed to her knees. The shouting men surrounded her. One wrapped her in a thick fur cloak and tossed her up over his shoulder. They carried her down to their dragon-headed ship before she understood what was happening.

The one who stole her seemed kindly enough. Over and over he spoke to her, but she understood nothing. On the third day he stroked his finger down her skin, and grabbed a handful of her silky hair, both as white as snowflakes. He stared into her face with eyes as glacier blue as her own, then pointed at her. "Frostbite." Her new name.

When they made camp, the Vikings wrestled and fought. Frostbite smiled. They reminded her of her Jotnar brothers back on the glacier, except for their small size and pinkish skins.

She was tiny as well, barely as tall as her human mother and not quite knee-high to the Jotnar. Her brothers considered her delicate, though neither heat nor cold would damage her. She inherited only a small measure of her father's magic: she could create enough fire to light a handful of sticks, she could freeze or melt a handful of flowers in an instant, and she could easily dig through snow and ice with her bare hands. A far cry from Ymir creating volcanoes through the ice and freezing huge swaths of land with a thought.

116

"Frostbite!" Her Viking called her back to the ship.

When they reached their destination, the village women took one look at Frostbite's hair and skin and backed away. "She cannot stay here," they muttered. "She is Ymir's daughter. The men are lucky she did not lure them to the glacier to freeze and be eaten by giants."

The women put a rope around her wrists and led her back to the men. "You must send her away. She is a danger to us all." A wrinkled woman spoke; the others nodding behind her.

Her Viking nodded in turn. "I will trade her for yellow amber." He let her keep the soft fur blanket.

The journey eastward lasted for months. Frostbite began to understand the language of the Vikings.

Her Viking stepped ashore. 'We come to trade."

Again, Frostbite did not understand the new language. It seemed that humans used a different language for each place they lived. She heard her name, along with the words "luck," "tribute," and '"Rus" before her Viking led her to an old woman with many clear yellow rocks.

The kindly old woman taught Frostbite to speak Rus, fed her, and taught her to cook and clean along with a dark-haired girl named Olga. Frostbite learned quickly, and often hummed the sounds of the northern winds to herself as she scrubbed.

"How can you be so happy?" Olga asked. "They're sending us to the northern forest in the spring. We're to serve Baba Yaga."

"Why are you scared? I would like to see the northern forests."

"Baba Yaga will eat us." Olga launched into stories about the witch. "…and her house runs about on chicken legs."

Frostbite scowled. She did not believe a word. *And what was a chicken?*

#

They trudged north into the forest accompanied by twelve strong Rus warriors. Frostbite ran to a tree, her arms outstretched. The tree must be eight or ten people's arms around. *A Jotnar-sized tree,* she thought and hundreds more ahead. Not like the tiny, twisted trees of her homeland. She could not wait to see the next wonder.

As the day wore on, the Rus began to mutter among themselves. A wolf howled in the forest, then another and another. The shadows beneath the trees oozed together into darkness.

Three wood gatherers ran into the camp. Snarls and growls echoed in the forest, and the fourth gatherer did not return. Night birds resumed their calls, and a few early insects buzzed against the night.

They built the fire up in front of the shelter, and both girls sat up all night watching the flames reflect yellow and red from a host of eyes on the other side. The eyes disappeared after the sun's weak rays penetrated the forest. They broke camp and continued walking.

When the sun reached its highest point, an odd cackling came from ahead. Two of the Rus went ahead to scout, then rushed back.

"We have found it."

They threaded their way along a trail between thick trees until they reached a clearing. Olga began to cry. Frostbite stood dumbfounded.

In the center of the clearing stood a small hut set up on two roughly cut poles with branches along the ground. The cackling noise, louder this time, came from the hut as first one pole, then the other, bent backwards and lifted. The hut walked around on giant bird legs! Perhaps Olga had some truth in her stories, after all. The door swung open, and another girl in her teens waved and leaned out.

"Welcome. I'm Elena, and Baba Yaga is expecting you. She will return before sunset." With that, the door closed again and the hut proceeded to walk in circles.

Well before the sun settled down, Frostbite heard a loud pounding from the sky. She looked up. A wrinkled old woman, blue as the Jotnar but merely human-sized, straddled a Jotnar cup. She pounded a wide-stick up and down in the center, crushing something. The cup flew through the sky. As it approached, Frostbite was again reminded of her Jotnar brothers by the woman's exceptionally long nose. This must be Baba Yaga.

"I smell Rus blood," Baba Yaga cackled. The hut jumped up and down in a frantic dance, cackling away with its owner. Baba Yaga motioned with her hand, and the hut settled to the ground. The door popped open again. Baba Yaga climbed off the cup and motioned to the girls. "Get inside." She walked in behind them and closed the door. The hut rocked as its chicken legs stood up and ran into the forest.

#

Elena showed the new girls what to do, taught them to say "Yes, Grandmother" and "No, Grandmother" when they addressed Baba Yaga, and gave them tips on how best to keep Baba Yaga happy. This last was their hardest task. The witch often screamed and beat the girls across their legs with a broomstick before locking them into cages at night: Elena at one end, Frostbite at the other, and Olga in the middle huddling in Frostbite's fur blanket.

On the third night, Frostbite waited until the witch fell asleep and whispered across the cages. "I wonder if we can escape."

Elena whispered back. "Our cages are magically locked, and she always catches up with those who run. When she returns with them, they are tossed in the stewpot."

"There is no way out?" Frostbite had already used a bit of her magic to light the cooking fire in the mornings, but

119

she did not think the other girls noticed. Try as she might, she could not think of a way for her magic to help her escape.

"Just before Midwinter's Eve, Baba Yaga will give one of us three tasks. If they are all complete by the third day, that girl is released and given a gift. Otherwise, it's into the stewpot!" A tear trickled down Elena's face.

Olga sat up. "The tasks are always impossible. Only two girls ever completed them."

"It is only springtime," said Frostbite. "We shall see what happens."

#

As the year progressed, Frostbite found her chores quite possible. She drew water, started cooking fires, and scrubbed the hut clean. Afterward, the girls picked wild garlic in season, medicinal herbs, and even wild strawberries.

Olga nudged Frostbite's arm, knocking her basket aside and spilling the tart berries. "Eat them while you can. In a few weeks they'll be gone, and we may not be here next summer." Berry juice stained Olga's lips and chin.

Frostbite picked up her fallen berries and rinsed them off. She gave a third to Baba Yaga, ate another third for supper, and saved the rest for breakfast.

When she woke, her empty basket lay on its side. Olga smiled with stained lips. When they went out to pick berries again, Frostbite stayed well away from Olga. After a few hours, she found a hollow in a tree trunk and picked a few large green leaves. She took two handsful of her berries, wrapped them in leaves, and froze them solid with her magic before stowing them inside the tree trunk. A fistful of damp leaves followed, also frozen. She returned with the other girls as evening approached.

Olga knocked the basket over again. "You didn't have much luck today."

"I'll share some of my berries with you," offered Elena.

120

"No need. I have just enough to eat tonight after Baba Yaga gets her portion."

Frostbite continued to save part of her strawberries each day. If she kept adding magically cold leaves inside the tree, the berries would stay frozen and she could have some every week for the whole year.

She added walnuts to her cache as well, when the season turned to fall and the snows began. Elena continued to teach them about everything edible and how to keep it through the winter.

"Can't you just show us the sugar trees in the spring?" Olga complained.

Elena burst into tears. "I have been here the longest. I will be the one Baba Yaga sends to do her tasks. I do not want to end in the stewpot!"

Frostbite touched Elena's hand. "You are a sweet girl, sharing everything with us. Perhaps Baba Yaga will set you free." Frostbite herself had no fear of the stewpot, for she knew its heat would not affect her.

#

Near Midwinter's Eve, the snows lay six feet deep and more in the forest, and the sun peeked out for only a few hours a day. Even the chicken legs of the hut struggled to move around the clearing. Frostbite walked in the forest each morning, collecting new fallen branches for firewood, and sometimes eating a single strawberry.

When Baba Yaga came to unlock their cages, she stopped in front of Elena's cage. "I have tasks for you, little one."

Elena stood silently, her eyes red from crying.

"Wait, Grandmother. I will do your tasks today." Frostbite stood at the front of her cage. "Baba Yaga, I will do your tasks." Elena whispered.

Baba Yaga stepped back and looked at the three girls. Elena stood bravely in spite of her misery, Frostbite stood calmly, and Olga huddled in the back of her cage, half-hidden by the warm-fur she stole from Frostbite on their first day.

"I think I will choose you." Baba Yaga unlocked Frostbite's cage and pulled her out. Elena moaned.

"I will give you three tasks: one today, one tomorrow, and one on the morning of the third day. By midnight on the third day, you must show me that the tasks are completed or I will cut you up and throw you into the stewpot." Her cackle set the chicken legs to hopping up and down.

Frostbite stood, stunned into silence by her growing fear. She had not considered that Baba Yaga would cut her apart. A small measure of magic she had, but it did not shield her from wounds nor grant her immortality. She took a deep breath. She could no longer change her mind.

Baba Yaga climbed onto her cup and threw open the hut's door. "Your first task is to draw water from the river and carry it back here with this." The witch tossed a sieve at Frostbite's feet. I will return at sunset." She flew into the air with a great pounding.

Frostbite stood at the door and looked back at the other girls.

Olga crept to the bars of her cage. "The stories," she whispered, "say to gather moss and mud and use them to line the sieve, then it will hold water."

Frostbite whispered her thanks, ignoring Olga's laugh behind her. She walked along the crusted snow to the river and dug deep through snow and ice. The river—and its mud—were frozen solid. Dead grasses long and yellow lay beneath the snow, but she found no moss.

"I could melt the river water, but with no moss, the water will run through. I have three days to think about it. I will figure it out." She returned to the hut just before Baba Yaga arrived.

"Where is my water?" demanded Baba Yaga.

"It is not yet the third day" Frostbite went willingly to her cage. The girls received no supper that night. After Baba Yaga fell asleep, Frostbite whispered of her failure to find moss.

Olga sneered. "You have been so quick to learn everything from Elena, but you cannot follow my simple instructions? You will land in the stewpot where you belong."

"Olga, you should not be so mean," scolded Elena.

#

The morning of the second day, Baba Yaga unlocked Frostbite's cage. "I want strawberries for dessert tomorrow after I've thrown you in the stewpot. Go find some in the woods:" She climbed onto her cup again, opened the door of the hut, and flew off with a great pounding.

"Ask the animals to find you a sheltered field," whispered Olga.

Frostbite whispered her thanks again as she left the hut. Even though she knew where her strawberry tree stood, she thought Baba Yaga would like fresh berries instead. After an hour she found a squirrel.

"Mr. Squirrel, can you please help me find fresh strawberries?"

The squirrel ran up a tree and chattered at her, tossing down small twigs that caught in her hair. She brushed them out as best she could with her fingers, then gathered the twigs up and put them in the tree with her frozen strawberries.

She set out into the forest again until she found a rabbit with fur as white as her own skin and hair.

"Mr. Rabbit, can you please help me find fresh strawberries?"

The rabbit twitched its nose twice, then ran into a willow thicket too dense for her to follow.

She continued on and soon found a fox, its fur nearly as white as the rabbit.

"Mr. Fox, can you please help me find fresh strawberries?"

The fox looked at her, raised its nose to sniff the air, and followed the rabbit into the willows.

She trudged back to the hut as the light faded, arriving again just before Baba Yaga.

"Where are my strawberries?" demanded Baba Yaga.

"It is not yet the third day." Frostbite walked into her cage and sat down.

Again Baba Yaga ate supper alone, and after the witch fell asleep, Frostbite whispered of her failure. "The animals would not speak to me."

"So you cannot magically speak to animals?" Olga sneered. "Do you at least have a magical doll to advise you? Or a special ring from your mother? How can you expect to escape with no magic? You are destined for the stewpot."

"Olga," Elena scolded again, "You should not be so mean."

Frostbite pondered Olga's words. If Baba Yaga expected magic to complete the tasks, then she would use her own small measure of magic. She thought long into the night.

#

On the third morning, Baba Yaga unlocked Frostbite's cage and then climbed atop her cup. "Today you will make me a rope of ashes." With that, she flew off, pounding away.

Elena's eyes brimmed with tears, "Why did you take the tasks from me? You will die tonight."

"We shall see." Frostbite reached through the bars of the cage and held Elena's hand.

"She is right," said Olga. "You will land in the stewpot tonight. There is no string or grass in the forest, nothing but snow and ice.

Frostbite took an apron with large deep pockets from the kitchen, as well as the sieve, and left the hut. She didn't need moss, and she already had strawberries.

Stopping at her strawberry tree, she put the twigs and frozen strawberries in separate pockets. Next she went to the riverside where she had dug for moss. Using her magic to help her dig through the snow, she plucked an armload of long, damp yellow grass.

She spent the next several hours braiding the grass into strings, and twisting the strings into a rope. With the last strand secured, she lay half the twigs out and made a small fire just hot enough to dry the rope. She coiled it up, and put it in the deepest, driest pocket of her apron. Her last task--or rather her first--became easy with her magic. She carved out a lump of river ice to fit in the sieve.

When the light faded, she returned to the hut. This time, Baba Yaga waited for her. Elena and Olga sat to either side of the witch, and the hut gleamed from a fresh scrubbing. Not a hair on the floor, nor an ash in the hearth remained.

"Where is my rope?" demanded Baba Yaga.

"Everything in its time, Grandmother." Frostbite rummaged in her apron pockets and brought out the sieve with its lump of ice first. "Here is your water."   '

"I cannot drink this."

Frostbite held a small pot beneath the sieve and used her magic. The water splashed down.

Baba Yaga accepted the pot and drank the water. "And my strawberries?"

Frostbite put the lump of frozen berries on a dish, and melted them clear of the ice. "You never said fresh strawberries. Here is your dessert, Grandmother."

Baba Yaga nibbled at the strawberries. "Very well. But where is my rope of ash?" She leaned over and tested the hearth with a hand. "There are no ashes here."

Frostbite pulled out the coil of braided grass and laid it out on the floor.

Baba Yaga leaned forward. "I see a rope, but it is not made of ash."

"Everything in its time, Grandmother." Frostbite took the remaining twigs from her pocket, laid them on the floor at one end of the rope, and started a small fire. The dry grass of the rope caught immediately. The fire raced down the rope, leaving nought but ash behind. "Your rope of ash."

"What?" Olga squawked. "That's not right."

Elena clapped quietly.

The hut shook as the chicken legs hopped up and down.

"Clever girl." Baba Yaga clapped her hands together. "You may ask for one thing to accompany your freedom."

"I would like the other tribute girls to be freed."

Olga sat silently with her mouth open.

Elena bowed to Frostbite and Baba Yaga. "Thank you," she whispered.

"There are two girls, which would be two things," Baba Yaga said as she stood. "I will allow you to take the polite one, the one who would have tried my tasks if you had not." She looked at Frostbite. "Where would you go?"

Frostbite thought, and then turned to Elena. "Where would *you* go?"

"Back to my aunt's house."

"Very well." Baba Yaga pounded twice on the floor and the chicken legs ran. The witch locked Olga back into the cage.

The hut stopped moving and the door popped open. Frostbite recognized the village where she learned to cook. Elena's aunt warmly greeted them, and they live there still unless they have moved on.

The Peasant's Lament

Another little mouth to feed,
Another mouth we didn't need,
But soon a pair of hands to weed,
And plow horse be his mighty steed.

Older daughters dally yet
With all young men who ask, and set
Their hopes that this be noble's get,
But on those hopes we cannot bet.

The Master's tithe is due too soon;
This year it falls on Harvest Moon.
Perhaps the lord will grant a boon
And leave enough to fill a spoon.

A peasant's back is sorely bent:
Enough to eat is his intent.
To feed the lords *our* grain all went.
This is truly our lament.

Colleen H. Robbins

The Tourney Game

A blaring of trumpets, procession of shields
Honor and Glory do march to the fields
Favors do fly from their helms and their belts
Soon many will leave here with bruises and welts
And again and again they look for the fame
To be found here... in the Tourney Game.

Honor opponents, honor your crown
Honor your lady (some spin all around)
And weapons are raised to the Marshalls so bold
Who shout out "Lay on!" and then again "Hold!"
And again and again they look for the fame
To be found here... in the Tourney Game.

A bout soon begins with the clashing of sword
Against armor and helmet of some love-struck lord
Who now dies a swift "death," and loudly complains
(At least 'til the ladies come care for his pains)
And again and again they look for the fame
To be found here… in the Tourney Game.

Crushed helms, broken shields, and snapped rattan swords
Fighters carried from the field on straight boards
The armorer cries, "So much for my store
Of loaner armor. I'll have to make more!"
And again and again they look for the fame
To be found here... in the Tourney Game.

Introduction to the Falcon Stories

In the time of King Arthur, the tales go, young Arthur pulled a sword from stone and became the first king of a united Britain. The son of Uther Pendragon, he was trained in combat by his foster family, and taught much more by the wizard Merlin (whose name means "falcon"). Arthur and Lancelot (a French knight) became friends and eventually started the Round Table in Camelot, where all member knights had an equal say.

There are many more stories of Arthur, but the drama includes magic, betrayal, and a final battle for succession between Arthur and his bastard son Mordred. Arthur was injured, and taken to Avalon, where he supposedly waits to return and save Britain.

The Falcon stories are based on a series of questions. What if Merlin were alive today and joined a medieval recreation group? What if the events he sponsored could bring you back in time to the actual Camelot? What if mistakes by modern people ended up in the legends?

Colleen H. Robbins

The Time of the Falcon

All things can get boring--even the SCA. Especially when the same old people in the same old groups hold the same old events year after year. Our group was like that until the Falcon joined.

You don't know about the Falcon? You really must be new. He joined about a year ago just before the strange things started happening. He's a short guy, somewhere in his 20s or 30s from the look of him, but no one's really sure. Yeah that's right, the thin one with a brownish beard. Now you remember. Well, he caused quite a stir when he first joined,

I can remember his first meeting. He walked in wearing a lumpy brown robe of coarse linen material, belted with a piece of faded linen. No, no one knows what he does for a living, but it sure must be tough sweaty work--he stank to high heaven. Anyway, our best costumer jumped all over him for not putting more effort into his costume. I think she accused him of being "unauthentic."

No, no, he didn't argue. He just took an incredibly old book out of his sleeve; so old it had real leather for a cover and hand-sewn pages covered in calligraphy. He opened it up to a real hand drawing of a costume exactly like his. The name under it was too smudged to be read, but the date, 294 Anno Domini, was clear. The name of the book? Some old latin book by someone named Ambrosius. No, I don't know for sure, I wasn't paying that much attention. You should've seen the look on the girl's face, she was absolutely floored.

He brought the heraldic device he wanted to the next meeting and talked with the herald. It was a pretty complicated picture; a diving falcon about to land on a rampant dragon, with all sorts of fancy stuff near the edges. It came back a month later, totally approved I might add. The heralds have never worked so quickly in their lives. You could tell the guy was new, he tried to put through Merlin as a name. Funny, huh? No, I don't remember what name he finally got approved. Everyone was calling him Falcon by then because of his shield. It just kind of stuck.

The strange things that happened? Oh, they didn't start for about two months. The first and only time Falcon went to fighter practice. No, he didn't get hurt. He made an especially good strike against his opponent—the squire it was--and the squire screamed and went down with a real sword slash in his arm. No, it healed up in no time, but Falcon decided not to be a fighter after that. I don't think they ever figured out exactly out what happened.

Next event it started happening to other fighters. You know, the rattan swords turning into steel in the middle of bouts. Yeah, the fighters thought so too--that's why they have two extra marshals to referee now, just to watch the swords.

No, the cars didn't start turning into dragons then— that happened a few months later. Right before Falcon started holding his own events. The first dragon? One of our best fighters walked towards his Porsche when it just *changed*. Sort of uncoiled into this big leering dragon, with smoke in its nostrils and everything. The color? Light blue, the same color as the car. The fighter took one look and backed up. He got about three steps before he tripped over a lance. Not one of those dinky things, a real lance. A big metal one with the three-foot leaf shaped blade and all. Well, yeah, it did have a six-foot oak handle. Anyway, the fighter charged the dragon; got it right through the neck, and ended up standing next to his Porsche, the lance all the way through the engine. A total loss. After the second time it happened, we learned you don't leave an event unless you ask Falcon first.

You didn't know? This isn't your first event here, is it? And no one's told you? Well, Falcon somehow managed to get this hall—and there's a lot more of it underground—for our constant use. Well, no, I'm not sure how he does it. One of our members thinks Falcon is involved in engineering as a mundane job, but that's another rumor and as to the one you brought up, it's true. Each weekend event, and yes we do have them every weekend here, seems to last a full year: No, of course you don't get any older, but you do see the local people age. No, they aren't mundanes. They really seem to have a medieval culture. No, they don't have plumbing or electricity, but we do. I'll show you how to turn the lights off later; it's all hidden. Falcon doesn't want the locals to learn about it. Power? Oh, we're over some sort of geothermal area--keeps the land warm like this all year round and makes a curtain of mist between our farmland and the local moors. It doesn't get too muddy out there, and all the trails are marked if you know what to look for.

If you ever get lost, don't talk about where you're from. The locals get real superstitious. Falcon says it's the way they say SCA. Sounds like "shay" or "shee," though I really don't understand what that has to do with anything. If you're lost? Well, if we don't notice any earlier, we'll find out at the end of the weekend and come back for you. Either way it's a chance to see medieval culture up close.

No, no—don't worry about medical problems. We've got a staff of six doctors here and a full surgical lab in the hall. I did mention that the hall is mostly underground, didn't I? We've got everything in there from a full kitchen, to the surgical lab, to a computer—320 terabytes--if that means anything to you. All the usual medieval stuff, too--a forge and smithy, grain mill, and all that. We do some trading with the local farmers, but yes, we're mostly self-sufficient.

That's right. Thank you for reminding me. We'll make-a quick stop at the tailor's to get you measured for costume patterns, and then I'll show you around your home-away-from-home.

Oh, did I forget? Falcon calls it Avalon.

Colleen H. Robbins

Falcon's Apprentice

Poor Lady Morgan. Such an untimely death, but I suppose she earned it. You didn't know her that well? That doesn't surprise me, especially these last few weekends.

Oh, yes, I did indeed. She first came here about a year ago. She used to run off on purpose just to stay with some of the peasants. No, no, her hair—natural straw blonde—she dyed her hair that awful black color. She was good at that sort of thing, and always so careful with her make-up.

I believe she was a college student—studying theatre if I remember right. You are too? Well, maybe you should listen and learn what *not* to do.

It all began when Lady Morgan met a prince on one of her jaunts, No, she didn't know he was a prince when he 'rescued' her from the moors. She didn't find that out until a few weeks later—that's Falcon's time, not ours. It's sometimes difficult to remember that each year here in Avalon is really just a weekend at home, thanks to Falcon. No, I still haven't found out how he does it, and I'm not planning to ask. Lady Morgan did that, and see where it got her.

In any case, Lady Morgan—her mundane name was Faye Delueca, though I really don't understand why you ask--Lady Morgan spent a number of local weeks pretending to be a serving wench at one of the inns. She found out quite a bit about her prince, but he left the area to go to some war somewhere. She pined for weeks.

The next weekend—our time--Falcon brought a local woman into the hall's surgical lab for her to have a baby. A little trouble at the birth, but nothing our doctors couldn't handle. Falcon sent her home the same day.

We kept the baby in an incubator for a few days until all danger was past, then Falcon brought him to a nearby

134

keep to be raised. We'd all visit him there every so often and call him Brown-Eyes. He had the most gorgeous brown eyes.

Lady Morgan? Oh, that's right. Forgive me. Well, Falcon discovered that same weekend that Lady Morgan sent a letter to her prince that spoke of the "shee"—that's how the locals pronounce S-C-A.

No, I don't think the letter she sent made it that far, and I'm not sure how Falcon discovered it. He banned Lady Morgan from Avalon for three months--that's our time— it was twelve or thirteen years by Falcon's time and we watched that little boy grow up.

Her prince? Oh, he died in a battle not long after the birth. He never even set eyes on the child. Really too bad— Falcon said the baby was his. In any case, the prince managed to hide the sword that Morgan's sister Vivianne gave him not too long before.

Vivianne? Oh, she's a short woman, though a bit taller than her sister. Yes, she's the one who constantly takes that little rebreather pack into the lake on the moors, She's a paleontology student, and claims that there are a wealth of fossils in the bottom of that lake.

The sword? A longsword, ornate yet functional, and made of chrome-steel alloy. Falcon suggested that she have two of them made, and then arranged for her to save one for the prince.

Regardless of her sister, Falcon sent Morgan   away for a time. Oh yes. She was as mad as a hornet for having missed so much. The baby was nearly grown, and ever so handsome. Dark brown eyes, hair to match, and a chuckling laugh that made everyone smile. Tall for a local, too.

No, Falcon never mentioned his name, but the boy used to call him "Merlin." Doesn't it figure? He couldn't get the SCA to pass the name, so he got a local to use it instead. And I'm told it means the same thing.

Well, Lady Morgan firmly attached herself to Falcon after that. They say he fell in love, and we saw them everywhere together. I understand he took her on as an apprentice and started to teach her some of his secrets. Morgan used to gloat about her 'knowledge', but never told us anything about it. In fact, before long she started to stay to herself an awful lot, at least until she saw the boy.

Did I say boy? Eighteen by then, and married. No, no children. And the boy had been crowned King several years before that. He even found his father's sword somewhere.

Oh, yes. Morgan. Well, she tried to lure him away from his wife, but it didn't work. I'm told she even managed to convince his wife to have an affair with Brown-Eyes' best friend, but I somehow doubt that. I could never picture that one doing anything to hurt his king.

I'm sorry—I guess my mind drifted a bit. Now where were we? Oh, yes. Did I tell you that Morgan had some skill with make-up? Well, she stood very near the queen's height and weight, and it didn't take too much for her to look like the Queen. Then the next thing you knew…

Well, yes, she *did* get pregnant. A boy, though she made everyone promise not to tell Falcon. A beautiful golden-haired boy who looked so much like his father. I believe she named him Mordred.

Oh, yes, he was very much like his father—including his aging. Lady Morgan got very upset when she realized that, but she sent him to live with a peasant family and did a lot of visiting.

Falcon found out about Mordred, but Morgan wouldn't tell him what she did with the child. So he barred her from Avalon for a second time—and this time it was permanent. Falcon remained very upset over the whole situation.

Unfortunately, Falcon had taught her too much. It didn't take Lady Morgan long to find her own way to Avalon, but by then Mordred had grown. A strapping young man with that golden hair so like his Aunt Vivianne's. Morgan seduced him, and didn't bother to tell Mordred that he was her son until after she became pregnant again.

Falcon's fury terrified everyone, especially after Morgan left Avalon to give her son "his rightful throne." And Brown-Eyes just thirty-eight. Falcon did something—no one knows what—but he changed things a little so that Morgan started to age like a local.

It took her two of our weekends to find out. Between that and the miscarriage, she became quite unhappy. And then she made her mistake.

On the field of battle, just as Mordred's forces were about to meet those who followed Brown-Eyes, Lady Morgan cheated some by arming her son's forces with superior weapons. Unfortunately for him, he only fielded a few hundred men to Brown-Eyes' thousand. A few of us went with Falcon to watch from a nearby hill. And to root for Brown-Eyes. I guess we all hoped he'd win.

It wasn't two hours before the battle when Lady Morgan walked out on the moors, muttering something about "changing the time flow." We couldn't see clearly, but her son helped her with whatever she did. I suppose she wanted to try and slow his aging as well. They stopped under an oak tree and bent over something. A moment later Morgan screamed and came running from beneath the tree.

Did I say running? She aged as she ran—a year for every step she took. Her son still followed her, but whatever they did, it didn't seem to affect him at all. She collapsed a few dozen feet away, dissolving to dust.

Oh, yes—that definitely demoralized Mordred. He still attacked, but too many of his men saw what happened. To put it mildly, they were routed.

Mordred? He and his father traded blows, with Brown-Eyes' sword slicing right through his son's fancy armor. Mordred got a good slice in on Brown-Eyes, too. A belly cut, nasty looking and bleeding something fierce. And somehow,

Brown-Eyes still managed to stand up, pull his sword from Mordred's body, and limp off toward our hill.

He wasn't at all surprised to see us. He merely turned and whispered "Fare Well" to his soldiers before falling unconscious at Vivianne's feet. Well, of course Vivianne was there. She kept track of her sister. Do you blame her?

Yes, we did take Brown-Eyes back to Avalon. Falcon muttered something about balancing the time frames. then he gave us the go-ahead.

Brown-Eyes was only in surgery for about six hours. And other than a brief bout of appendicitis or something as a complication; all went well. Vivianne spent every minute with him that she could while he was getting well. In fact, Brown-Eyes proposed to her.

Of *course* that's the same Vivianne who got married last month. And his lack of legitimate children was his first wife's fault—Vivianne just found out she's pregnant. And Falcon says that this child will be SCA-normal. Arthur can't wait--he's hoping for a son.

The Broken Sword

Isn't little Dan such a beautiful boy? They say he looks a little like his half-brother Mordred did with that golden hair. Arthur is so pleased that he's already planning to give Dan his sword as soon as the boy's old enough.

The sword? Yes, It's one of the two chromium-steel alloy blades that Vivianne ordered-- with Falcon's permission, I might add. She carries the one that was once broken. You can see the mend if you look closely.

You never heard about the broken sword? You've missed a lot of the legends—and an awful lot of history. Oh, I understand. You've just moved to the area; You'll like it a lot, especially the weekly events here in Avalon.

Vivianne? She's a paleontology student, going for her Master's degree I believe. She's found a number of fossils in the bottom of the lake on the moors. I understand that she's even found a connecting passage between the lake and one of the cooler springs here, Yes, she's the one who carries that rebreather. No, it's solid pack. Vivianne says that all Marine Paleontologists use them to prevent chemical back-up. I expect she'd know.

The broken sword? Vivianne ordered them from one of our armorers a few months after Falcon asked him to make a set of plate mail of that same alloy. He gave it as a gift to some local a distance away—in France, I believe.

Vivianne had the swords made to be identical. She used to joke that she should give one to her husband when she chose him, but Falcon convinced her to give one to a prince that her sister was involved with instead.

No, she didn't marry him. He died a short time later. Everyone looked for the sword, but it wasn't found until Brown Eyes--that's what we called Arthur—was twelve or thirteen years old. That's local years, mind you. We age a lot slower than the locals.

Arthur broke the sword. Vivianne was diving in the lake looking for fossils when it happened. She noticed Arthur and another knight jousting on a field near one end of the lower bridge, so she took time to watch.

After the first pass, Vivianne became positive of one thing. Between the way Arthur's lance shattered on the knight's armor, and the distinct accent the knight spoke with, the armor the foreign knight wore had to be the same set that Falcon took to France.

Arthur was slightly more skilled than the foreign knight, but the armor made the bout equal. When the two drew swords, Vivianne held her breath. She expected the next part to be messy.

Vivianne told me later that she seriously considered using the second sword to go and help; but she didn't have time to more than draw it. Arthur swung--a similar blow to the one he later used to kill Mordred, according to Vivianne— and sparks flew. Arthur's sword broke in two, but not before it went through the French Knight's armor.

No, it didn't kill him, but the French knight went over backwards and just lay there. From what I understand, the sword barely scratched him. There wasn't much blood at all, but both boys went into shock. Yes, boys. They couldn't have been more than fourteen or fifteen years old, and Arthur already crowned King. But both went into shock-- Arthur because the unbreakable sword   broke and the French knight because the armor that couldn't be scratched was cut through.

Arthur became so upset about killing the French knight that he threw the pieces of his sword into the lake and shouted some nonsense about giving up the throne. Without even an heir to take it!

And of course he looked at the lake just in time to see Vivianne standing in waist-deep water with her sword all whole. His sword, he probably thought. The poor boy barely managed to kneel. Vivienne felt so sorry for him that she handed him her identical sword.

The French knight chose that moment to groan, and Vivianne slipped her rebreather back on as Arthur turned away. When he looked back she had vanished without a bubble in sight.

What happened to Arthur? He weathered a number of problems and went on to unify much of the area. His bastard son Mordred later challenged him for the throne. Arthur managed to be in the right place at the right time when Mordred's mother unbalanced the time frame. To set it right, Falcon adopted Arthur into Avalon, and Arthur married Vivianne not long after. Now they have young Dan.

Oh, I see you've heard about him. Yes, he and his young friends ran off to Ireland this past summer. You wouldn't think a five-year-old child could get into so much trouble, though it's cute how he calls himself Dan of the SCA.

How much trouble? Well, it's going to be a long time before the Irish stop talking about the people—Tuatha in their tongue—of Dan.

NBMB Extra Copyright Pages

"The Dragon's Quest," The Nottinghill Quill, March 1980.

"The Last Unicorn," The Nottinghill Quill, May 1981.
"The Lure," Wordeater (literary magazine of Joliet Junior College), no. 109, (spring 2001).
"The Mermaid," The Nottinghill Quill, Aug/Sep 1980.
"The Peasant's Lament," The Nottinghill Quill, March 1982.

"The Scribe's Forgotten Pen," The Nottinghill Quill, July 1981.
"The Time of the Falcon," The Runes, Vol.1, Issue 1, 1982.
"The Tourney Game," The Runes on the Mountain, May 1982.

"The Trek to the Hidden Mountain," The Runes: Arts and Sciences, March 1983.
"Ugly Horses," Write Where We Are: Write On Joliet Anthology 2018.
"Unicorns Rear Up," The Nottinghill Quill, March 1981.
"Whispering Robes," The Nottinghill Quill, Aug/Sep 1980.

ACKNOWLEDGEMENTS AND THANKS

As usual, there are so many people to thank: my family, so many old friends who wanted to see many of these stories and poems reprinted, and the ones who encouraged me to put some in print for the first time. A few stand out. My granddaughter Mara, who at seven asked to read "Ugly Horses." Her comment afterward: "Grandma, I prefer my unicorns to be vegetarian." Thank you to Cherish Hunter, who read an early version of the rainbow story years ago, and specifically asked for it to be in this collection. It took some digging to find it, but here it is.

These stories and poems might never have been so readable if it weren't for my teachers at Lewis University (Romeoville, IL), and Jeanne Cavelos, Director of the Odyssey Fantasy Writing Workshop (Manchester, NH). My classmates at Odyssey and the TNEO reunion workshops helped as well. So many people read and commented on earlier versions of the stories that I don't have room to name them all, but Susan Abel Sullivan helped me so much,

Thank you to Carol "Gennie" O'Connor, who encouraged me to submit poetry to The Nottinghill Coill so many years ago, and to Shannon who edited The Runes on the Mountain.

And of course, Thank You to Tom Hernandez and Denise Baran-Unland, our fearless leaders of the Write On Joliet group in Joliet, IL, who continue to encourage me to write "homework" pieces and read certain other pieces aloud every year. Someday I'll get over my fear of public speaking. Thank you to the ever-growing membership of WOJ, many of whom have commented on my stories. And a special thank you to Duanne Walton, who videotapes our yearly "open mic" readings and puts them on his You Tube site.

https://youtube.com/user/4thtroika

I've got several stories up there, including a few from this collection. Thank you all again! -CHR

About the Author

Colleen H. Robbins has been writing since she was nine years old and holds a BA in English Language and Literature from Lewis University. She has attended numerous workshops including the Iowa Summer Writer's Conference (2003), the six-week long Odyssey Fantasy Writer's Conference (2007), and TNEO (2009, 2013). Her stories, poems, essays, and articles have appeared under a variety of names in everything from small regional magazines to the rpg-gaming oriented magazines <u>Different Worlds</u> and <u>The Dragon</u>, and have been included in numerous anthologies. She writes both mainstream (literary) fiction and genre (Science fiction, fantasy, and horror).

Outside of writing, Colleen lived in numerous (mostly coastal) states, and spent her childhood reading, primitive camping, hiking, skiing, and sailing in the northeastern United States. She joined the Society for Creative Anachronism [recreating Medieval and Ancient Times], learned the broadsword and round shield fighting style, and took up archery, bellydance [Egyptian / Turkish style, then added American Tribal], costuming, and motherhood while in the southeastern US. Further moving around the country allowed her to visit numerous caves and mines, fossil sites, and historical sites such as Gettysburg. She enjoys attending historical re-enactment weekends of a number of eras and cultures, and is a past member of the Historical Miniatures Gaming Society. She continues to add new experiences such as surfing and knife-throwing. Many of her experiences and travels find their way into her writing.

Colleen H. Robbins

Colleen has worked as a Paralegal, Medical Records Analyst, Bellydance Instructor, and Library Volunteer, among other jobs, and holds degrees from the University of South Florida (Tampa, (FL), Joliet Junior College (Joliet, IL), and Lewis University (Romeoville, IL).

Upcoming:

Ciara's Island: a Daraga novel

When Nicholas and Alaan are swept away in the currents from Rockhold, they wash up somewhere along the northern shore. Nicholas has been injured and lost his magic; Alaan has been captured.

Red-haired Ciara, brought up by dragons, is running from the insane dragon that attacked her mother. Travelling with unhatched eggs, she and her sister encounter first Nicholas, then Alaan.

But can Nicholas and Alaan shepherd a teenaged dragon and a handful of hatchlngs to the Eastern lands and the Dragon Valley fast enough to avert a new crisis?

Invasive Species and Other Light Horror
(a short story collection)

How do you exorcise a fish?

Working for the Christmas Demon? Not all it's cracked up to be.

If the demons win, what will life be like?

Colleen H. Robbins

###

www.ingramcontent.com/pod-product-compliance
Lightning Source LLC
Chambersburg PA
CBHW051833170626
46807CB00003B/1162